Legends Of Omnia – Volume I

Table of Contents

CHAPTERS

Omnia's World Map

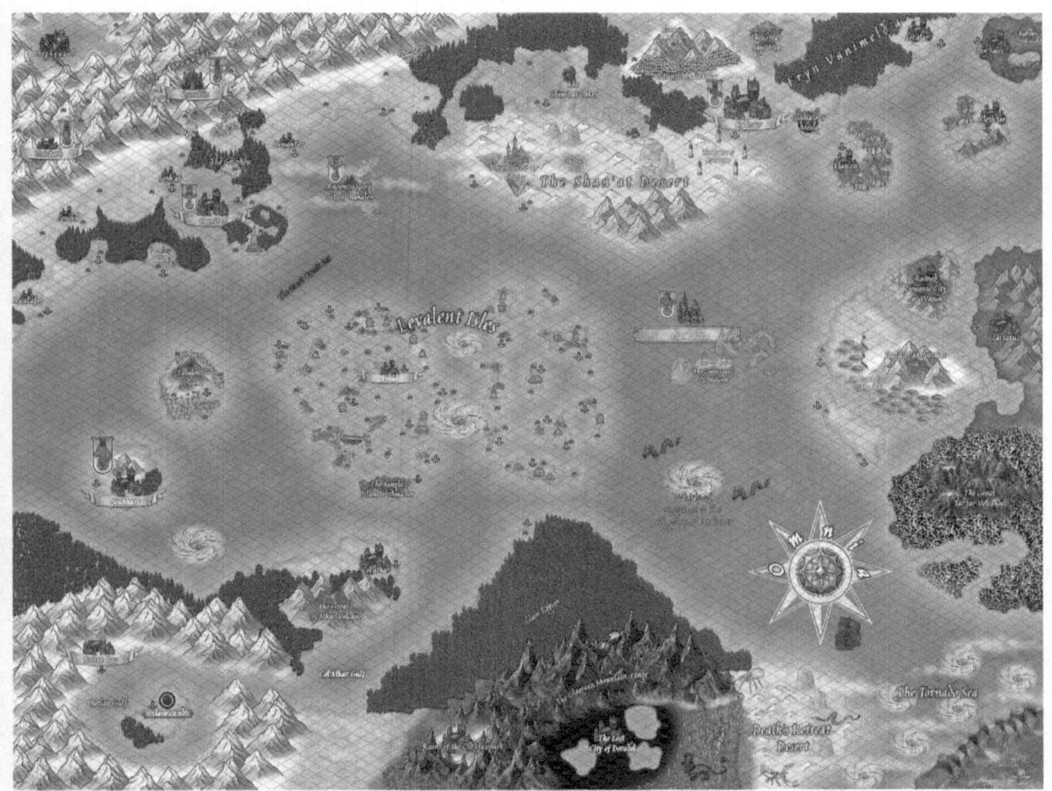

WORLD INFO

Name: OMNIA

Races: Humans, Elves, Dwarves, Harrim, Scultar, Gnome, Dragons, Demons, Celestials, Mermaid / Merman.

Gods, Deities and Demons of Omnia

Initially, out of the nothingness and emptiness of space, a bright burst of light emerged and an ultimate being came into existence. This ultimate being named itself Aval'es, Aval'es drifted into the emptiness of space alone for millennia. He started creating worlds and universes, making stars collide just to ease its boredom.

Aval'es then decided that it would create more beings with great power and let them populate the vastness of space. He would go to create 12 Divine beings and bestowed them with near limitless powers. After he created them, he took a step back to see what they would do in the cosmos and hoped they would entertain the boredom he felt. He also chose to hinder his ability to see the future and just watch for his entertainment, as if someone knows what's going to happen, there's no fun in that and since the whole reason he did everything was out of boredom, he sealed his ability to see the future by ripping out his left eye.

These Divine beings were the Gods who would eventually create the world of Omnia, all of its animals, creatures, and races.

All twelve of these divine entities evolved into Aspects of Greatness.

The Aspects are divine beings that exist outside of the physical and spiritual realms.

These beings never saw themselves as good or evil; in fact, they appeared to be neutral for the first millennia that they guarded Omnia and the Cosmos. Their abilities were nearly limitless, but only three of them were the most powerful.

The three that would eventually take up the mantles of the Aspects of Life, Death and Time, they were the most powerful of all the Aspects. These Aspects would create everything, all the worlds, realms and planes were created by them and they would only have one rule, one principle between them. That principle would be to "Never meddle in the affairs of the mortal races they created".

The millennia passed and the Aspects were fascinated by the living beings in the world of Omnia. Out of all the worlds they had created, the mortal races in Omnia seemed to be the most intelligent of them all and even had a concept of Deities that they would come to worship and request guidance, assistance and in some cases even request vengeance on their enemies from.

Some of the Aspects slowly began to change as they gained more worshippers from the mortal races they had created. Some even sought to protect their faithful during times of conflict, to aid them during times of famine, and so came to be worshipped as Gods by the mortal races, and with each worshipper they gained or each sacrifice that was being made to their name, they were further empowered.

That was a violation of their sole principle: "**Never meddle in the affairs of the mortal races they created**".

As a result, a war broke out between them. They soon came to create the immortal race known as Celestials to fight in their conflict. The Aspects' behaviours, appearances, and even beliefs would eventually change during that Great Aspect War, and after centuries of fighting amongst themselves and wreaking havoc in the realm of Omnia, they would try to form a pact to end the conflict because as it would appear, it was a stalemate.

They turned to the strongest among them, those who did not take sides nor participated in the War, and those that remained "**pure**" in their beliefs, forms, and behaviours.

The Aspects of Life and Death and Time, Leandra, Demiur and Chrominia, were the only ones who did not participate in the Incomparable Aspect Conflict; a conflict did not interest them in the least.

The other Gods turned to them to form a pact to end all hostilities between them.

And so they gathered all the Gods beyond the Great Gate, to the realm they had created for the souls of Omnia's mortal beings.

When they were all gathered, they agreed to halt the fighting but not to renew their original pact which was to never meddle in the affairs of mortals, they were all enjoying the newfound power they were getting from their worshippers and didn't want that to stop.
They all agreed to leave behind an Avatar of each one to look after the mortal races so they could retire to their own Domain and continue their eternal lives in peace. The decision would be unanimous since all of them agreed.

All but one, Malekus, the God of War, had different ideas.

He openly opposed this idea with the other divine beings, telling them that if he were made Lord of the Godly beings, he would, in effect, put an end to all harm, but his request was denied. Because the other Divine beings were tired of fighting and refused to listen to or fulfil Malekus' demands, and that was when The God of War attacked, fighting in blinding speeds but his skirmish would be cut short. Demiur stepped in and asked him to lay down his weapons and surrender as the decision had already been made, he could either follow the rest or suffer the consequences of his disobedience.

Malekus once again refused, and charged, attacking Demiur head on this time. The two Gods fought day and night for days, Malekus seemingly stronger than ever before, probably all the conflicts and wars that had erupted in the world of Omnia were fuelling him with even more power and he was very close to being on par with Demiur's power. The God of Death would not entertain him any longer though, he pleaded with him again to cease this pointless fight and submit, even though he had taken up the Aspect of Death, Demiur was not keen on taking Malekus' life. He pleaded one last time for Malekus to lay down his arms and submit or he would have to use the full extent of his power and that might even kill the God of War.

Malekus once again denied his pleas and charged head on only to be met by Demiur's palm over his face, dragging him down from the skies of Omnia, to smash him into the biggest mountain of the world, creating the Great Tar'tar Volcano.

Malekus was finally defeated but not dead, Demiur once again held back his full strength in order not to kill his brother.

It was at this moment that all the Celestials that followed Malekus would have a drastic shift in their appearance. Instead of the white feathery white wings they had, new terrible black bat like wings replaced them as they fell down in pain and suffering while their appearances changed while their lord was being imprisoned and they were losing their connection with him.
The once beautiful Celestials of War of Malekus were now the damned Demon race, hideous and grotesque they looked like the stuff of nightmares. Many perished during their "change", the rest gathered their remaining forces and withdrew to the city of Wajun that would later be come to be known as Demonic City of Wajun.
After witnessing their transformation, the Gods decided to exile them to another plane of existence which would soon come to be called "The Demonic Realm".
They shifted the Demonic City of Wajun and made it transparent leaving the doorway to the Demonic Realm where within the transparent image of the once great city.

The Gods came to an agreement and chose to restrain Malekus and bind him to the Soul Domain outside the Great Gate, where he could not incite conflict over mortal races, or so they thought.

They imprisoned him in an impervious shell that would hold him forever, and the other Gods cursed it, "This prison could never be unlocked by anything more than a mortal" because the other Gods knew that imprisoning Malekus in the Soul Domain would mean that no mortal would ever reach this place to free him, so they left him with this ironic sense of hope.

The other Gods had no idea that many souls pass to the Soul Domain while still alive, sort of like an astral projection of their soul. Malekus knew this because he witnessed dying soldiers' souls leaving their bodies and travelling to the Soul Domain, and their brothers in arms healing them and forcing their souls back into their bodies. This would be the catalytic information he would need to have hope.

Malekus knew that this would not stop the battles on Omnia, and that his Celestials of War would continue to do his bidding, so unable to do anything else, he chose to accept his fate, wait until his time comes again, and sow seeds of his control in the hope that one day he will be liberated and able to exact his vengeance on the Divine beings that chained him to this damned place and claim their power for himself.

And once he'd dealt with them and absorbed their powers, he'd be ready and strong enough to take on both Leandra and Demiur at the same time and become the ultimate being in the Universe, or so he thought as unbeknownst to him, Aval'es was the most powerful being.

He waited patiently, and eventually some mortals made it to the Great Gate without dying; this was his chance, this was what he had been waiting for to make his move. He planted the seeds of his power within them, sealing their magic. These mortals' ability to use magic was lost when they returned to their bodies. Furthermore, if these mortals had children, their descendants would eventually develop a strange crimson power, the power of the God of War.

He sowed his power on these souls in hope that their offspring's might be able to set him free, if they died, they just weren't worthy of his grace and his power would just be transferred back to him. After all, Divine power always goes back to its owner unless it is taken from another being with Divine power.

This power could manifest as shields, swords, pole-arms, chains, and other types of weapons of war, as well as an increase in the user's physical prowess such as strength, speed, endurance, and fortitude.

This was **Malekus's** power; no one knew what was happening to these children, and some of them were imprisoned, killed, or worse, had their souls ripped from them as sacrifices for Gods.

Malekus knew he'd have to wait centuries, if not millennia, for a worthy "**child**" to appear, one that could wield his full power that was fragmented and scattered throughout the millennia that he has been a prisoner, but he could wait because his vengeance meant everything to him, and he wanted to calculate everything and leave nothing to chance.

Malekus' children could also take power from one another in combat by usually killing each other or by forfeiting it, with the strongest one taking the power of the defeated and further bolstering his own and thus making them gradually ascend to a higher state, allowing them to venture beyond the Great Gate much like their parents did, but they would have to be fully alive and eventually free Malekus.

Throughout the centuries, many mortals realised what this strange power was and sought others to defeat and further strengthen themselves, but no one came close to ascending to free him from his prison.

Once a wielder of **Malekus'** power dies from anything other than by the hand from another power wielder, the power leaves them at the Soul Gate and becomes one with **Malekus** once again.
Malekus has calculated that in order for a child to be able to free him, they would need to gain **100** fragments of his power in order to do so.
Malekus also sent out a **special** fragment of his power and made it so that this fragment would only seek **wise** mortals and bestow upon them the knowledge of the fragments. He did so that his children would be able to seek whomever possessed the **Knowledge Fragment** as he called it and learn more about their ultimate mission of freeing him.
This special fragment however did not give any kind of special powers or skills like the rest of the fragments gave their hosts, it gave him **knowledge** and an extension on his **lifespan** so that he or she would be able to **guide** his children towards their ultimate goal.
Once the **Knowledge Fragment** host dies, the fragment seeks the next host on its own without ever having to pass the **Soul Gate** and return to **Malekus**.

The 12 Aspects

Leandra took over the Aspect of Life and became the **Goddess of Life**.
Leandra takes the shape of an Elven maiden with long golden hair and glowing golden eyes in a white dress.

Demiur took over the Aspect of Death becoming the **God of Death**.
Demiur takes the shape of a Dark Elf with white hair and glowing white eyes dressed in an all-black outfit often carrying a scythe on his back.

Tyron took over the Aspect of Justice becoming the **God of Judgement**.
Tyron takes the shape of a Dwarven Legendary warrior with brown hair and glowing golden eyes in a Golden Armour carrying a golden hammer and axe.

Malekus took over the Aspect of War becoming the **God of War and Conflict**.
Malekus takes the shape of a Human Warlord with grey hair and glowing black wearing a silvery spiked black armour carrying a Great sword in his back.

Lyc took over the Aspect of Lies becoming the **Goddess of Lies and Deceit**.
Lyc takes the shape of a Mermaid with black hair and glowing teal eyes often described as a siren, as like her, Sirens use Deceit to lure their victims to their death.

Saeth took over the Aspect of Suffering becoming the **Goddess of Suffering and Pain**.
Saeth takes the shape of a Dark Elven Maiden with white hair and glowing yellow, clad in leather straps with inward

spikes that poke into her body causing immense pain which she seems to be constantly enjoying.

Chrominia took over the Aspect of Time becoming the **Goddess and Keeper of Time**.
Chrominia takes the shape of an Elven maiden with white hair and glowing golden eyes wearing a golden cape with a cowl that hides most of her hair and facial features and always carries a Silver and Golden hourglass in her hand.

Abaelat took over the Aspect of Agony becoming the **God of Agony and Despair**.
Abaelat takes the shape of a Human warrior with black hair and glowing white eyes, clad in a leather armour with two longswords on his back and many daggers decorating his armour all over starting in his forearms and ending in his calves.

Satelab took over the Aspect of Salvation becoming the **God of Salvation and Redemption**.
Satelab takes the shape of a Dwarven Elder with white hair and glowing white eyes, simple clothes and he is usually carrying a walking stick in his hands.

Comalaet took over the Aspect of Destruction becoming the **God of Destruction and Ruination**.
Comalaet takes the shape of an anthropomorphic animal, usually a Lion much like the Harrim with a long golden mane and glowing red eyes.

Sigamunt took over the Aspect of Creation becoming the **God of Creation and Inventions**.
Sigamunt takes the shape of a Dwarven Blacksmith with black and white hair and glowing golden eyes, clad in a Blacksmith's outfit often seen with ash and burns on his face and hands, always carrying a blacksmith hammer.

Devant took over the Aspect of Damnation becoming the **God of the Damned and Doomed**.
Devant takes the shape of a Half-Elf with brown hair and glowing yellow eyes, wearing a full plate armour wielding a huge burning katana which burns in a black flame on one hand and a smaller with a void aura around it on the other.

3 Neutral Aligned Aspects

The Aspect of Life

The Aspect of Death

The Aspect of Time

4 Good Aligned Aspects

The Aspect of Justice

The Aspect of War

The Aspect of Salvation

The Aspect of Creation

5 Evil Aligned Aspects

The Aspect of Lies and Deceit

The Aspect of Suffering and Pain

The Aspect of Damnation and Doom

The Aspect of Destruction and Ruination

The Aspect of Agony and Despair

Malekus cast a "**Curse of War**" on the other God's creations, their Celestial forces they were created during their War of the Aspects, and thus the Great Conflict was born, in which the Celestials would fight each other in an unending conflict inflicting havoc across Omnia, as War and Conflict would fuel his powers wherever he may have been, even while imprisoned.

When the Gods saw their creation in ruins, they bestowed the gift of Magic on the mortal races, allowing them to finally defend themselves from the war before retiring to the Soul Realm.

They would also create Avatar's with their powers in order to keep the balance in the world they had created while they would be gone. The Avatars of Life and Death, Leandra's and Demiur's, would assist Omnia's creatures' souls in crossing over to the Gods' realm, where the Avatar of Tyron would judge them and decide who would be worthy of being returned.
These three Avatars looked humanlike with Death's Avatar wearing a long black hooded robe, carrying a big black book covered with bonelike features which was his list of who to collect to guide to the afterlife, his face wasn't visible through the hood but his hands looked skeletal.
The Avatar of life looked like a humanoid with more feminine features, a white dress and it looked like its skin was made out of pure light while someone could notice the golden hair it had.
Lastly, the Avatar of Tyron looked like a seasoned bearded Human in his early 50's, with a golden armour gleaming with a soothing golden light.

The worthy souls would be given another chance at life and reincarnated as another creature, whereas the unworthy would fuel the Great Beyond, the Great Gate through which the Gods entered this Universe or traversed to the Soul Domain. The Great Beyond would receive and consume a constant flow of souls, creating new ones with the combined power of the Gods, which would eventually be born as creatures in our Universe.

Aval'es was watching all along and came to like the mortal beings of Omnia, he was glad for creating the Divine beings and thought that it was time for him to travel to the world of Omnia and experience what it had to offer in the form of a mortal.
And so he did, he started walking the world seemingly as a mortal with no one knowing who he really was by taking the guise of a frail old man, not even the great Divine beings he created that were being revered as Gods in the world of Omnia.
Aval'es took the disguise of an old man wearing an eye-patch on his left eye, in a dark blue robe with a big white beard and a walking stick to "**aid**" him while traveling. He had a spell book bound on one side hanging off his belt and several potions of the other side and a knapsack on his back. Seemingly a traveling wise-man in his early 60's, sturdy enough for his years and the wrinkles around his eyes betrayed the wisdom gained throughout his years.
He travelled for centuries and gathered more information about this world that his unknown servants created and tried to enjoy himself while occasionally teaching the mortal races about the world and his encounters in his travels without ever revealing his true identity, he seemed to be amused by their hunger to learn and he tried to satisfy that hunger. Along his travels he noticed that the mortals longed to believe in higher powers in order to explain things in their daily lives that didn't make sense to them and thus they "made up" new deities to believe and even though they weren't real they chose to worship them, this gave Aval'es an idea. Since the mortal races had that need, he made it so if enough people believed in a God, this God would come into being out of nothing. That would be more amusing for him.

And thus new Gods were created in Omnia over the centuries. These Gods would either be beings that came into existence simply because mortal races believed they existed and worshipped them, thus creating them, or mortals who excelled in some way and other mortals began worshipping them, making their magic stronger, much like how worship works in the Gods, and they eventually attained Godhood but were nowhere nearly strong the **12** original deities of Omnia.
Even though we know which deities were created thus far, only Aval'es knows the exact number and powers of these deities. Aval'es curiosity wasn't only as to how many deities would be created by the beliefs of mortal races but also

what would the Greater Deities, the Aspects would do about it. Would there be another Godly war on the way? Would they accept them?

New Gods & Deities

Elpir, God of Spells and Magic - Elpir was one of the Gods who appeared out of nowhere simply because mortals thought he existed. Because everyone in Omnia possesses magical abilities, everyone believes in Elpir, making him one of the Major Gods in Omnia's Pantheon.
Elpir is considered to be a **Greater Power** God.

Eira, Goddess of Healing - Eira was a Half-Elf healer who worked as a cleric for Leandra and spent her life healing the sick and wounded. She was pursued and tortured by Elves until Leandra took pity on her and granted her Godly powers to serve as one of her Avatars, the Avatar of Healing.
Eira is considered a **Medium Power** Goddess.

Nechtan, the God of Water - Nechtan was a wonderful young Merman. He spent his entire life in Atalante, working as a trader between the various underwater tribes. During his life, he helped a lot of Humans and Harrim because he saw too many shipwrecks and saved their sailors, who eventually thought he was a God of the Sea and was saving their lives. He gained a following among land dwellers who believed he was a God, so he eventually became one and assumed the title of God of the Sea and Water.
Nechtan is considered a **Major** God.

Vecnir, God of Death – Vecnir was originally a very talented wizard from the Glaor Region that eventually became corrupt by his usual use of Necromancy and eventually turned himself into a Lich. After wreaking havoc he earned the nickname Deathbringer as whoever met him in battle, was doomed to die and have their souls absorbed. His name is also associated to rituals, sacrifices and power stealing.
Vecnir is considered a **Major** God.

Fortuneiv, Goddess of Luck & Fate – Fortuneiv came into being by the strong beliefs of the mortals that are addicted to gambling and believe that lady luck is with them, worshipping her to bring them luck and gain fortunes while gambling.
Fortuneiv is considered a **Medium Power** Goddess.

Aither, Aural and Zephyt, the 3 Gods of Winds and Skies – A lot of merchants and travellers worship the trio of wind Gods in the world of Omnia, mainly praying to them before a trip by water or air to bring favour them with their winds for a quick and safe arrival.
Although all three of them are lesser Gods, they've gaining followers in travellers and merchants steadily.
They are considered to be **Medium Powered** Gods.

Luminia, Goddess of the Night and the Moon – Luminia is the personification of the moon as a goddess. She was worshipped at the new and full moons. Usually having sacrifices take place during full moons.
Luminia is a **Major** Goddess.

Solton, God of the Sun – Solton is the God of the sun, mainly revered everywhere around the world of Omnia.
An ancient prophecy that its origins are lost in time suggests that at the reckoning of the world, the twilight of the Gods will come and Solton will be one of the last remaining Gods, if he falls, the whole world of Omnia falls into darkness.
Solton is a **Major** God.

Satkasi, God of Pleasures, enjoyment, and delight – Satkasi came into being very recently as the mortal races of Omnia started enjoying themselves more and more and were valuing the delights of enjoying themselves and having a good time.
He is one of the lowest **Lesser** Gods.

Deities and their Off-springs

Some of the Greater Aspects and New Gods eventually grew closer over the centuries and had children, some of their children would share some of their power or manifest completely new powers of their own and some would be revered as Deities themselves while others would seek other things in life.

Children of the Aspects

Leandra – Demiur → Cain – Abbalon
Tyron – Chrominia → Ellysa – Totenmus - Zoeth
Abaelat – Saeth → Avernus – Syvael – Mortulak

Cain : Cain was the one of the two sons of Leandra and Demiur, born at the same time with his brother Abbalon only seconds after his brother, he inherited a considerable amount of his parents powers. He felt jealous of his brother for having slightly more powers than him ever since they were born. He can be considered on the same level an Aspect but not on the same level of power as his parents.
Abbalon : Abbalon was the firstborn son of Leandra and Demiur, only preceding his brother by mere seconds but that gave him the advantage in terms of power as he has the combines powers of his parents to a certain extent. He can be considered to on the same level of power as an Aspect but not on the same level of power as his parents.

Ellysa : Ellysa is the eldest daughter of Tyron and Chrominia, a gentle soul that has the combined powers of both her parents but doesn't really like to use them. Ellysa had the unique power of prophecies. She could see visions of the future that not even her Mother, the **Mistress of Time** could predict (as there are an infinite amount of possible futures depending on everyone's choices and actions) and that made her a one of a kind Goddess among Gods. Even though she had this incredible power, Ellysa sought to have a normal life among the mortal races and took the form of a Human girl in order to blend in within their society and live a normal life. No one has seen her for centuries. She was considered to be above the level of a Major God, just below the level of that of an Aspect.
Totenmus : Totenmus was the middle child of Tyron and Chrominia and had the combined powers of his parents with his Father's powers being a bit more prevalent. He decided to build himself a temple where the mortal races could worship him and his followers would pass down judgement in mortal squabbles, much like his father's Dogma. Totenmus is considered to be on the same level as that of a Major God.
Zoeth : Zoeth was the youngest sibling of the 3 and youngest daughter of Tyron and Chrominia. She has the combined power of her parents with her Mother's powers being a bit more prevalent. She is a little bit of a trickster and likes to play pranks on mortals for her own amusement. She doesn't like the idea of being worshipped like her brother and the only way she interacts with mortals is through her pranks. Zoeth's powers are considered to be on the same level as that of Major Gods.

Avernus : Avernus is the firstborn son of Abaelat and Saeth, he was the first of the Aspect offspring's that interacted with the mortal races as he liked seeing them suffer, he chose to live his life among the mortal races, always hiding his powers but slightly influencing the mortals around him causing pain and suffering. Throughout his life he always liked to take the role of a torturer in order to inflict the maximum amount of pain as that was his sadistic idea of fun. This had to be stopped eventually by Eira as she couldn't stand seeing this much suffering anymore. They battled out for days and eventually with the power of Elpir, she won and demanded his surrender and for him to leave mortals alone. His powers were a combination of his parent's powers and he was considered to be on the level of a Major God.
Syvael : Syvael was the middle child of Abaelat and Saeth, she did combine the power of both her parents but did not like to use her Godly powers at all. Even though she was the middle child, her powers were greater than those of her siblings which made them angry and jealous towards her, even more when she clearly stated that she didn't like to use her powers. Eventually Syvael left to never be seen again, joining the mortal world and hiding her powers from everyone. Her powers were said to be above the level of a Major God, nearly close to those of an Aspect.
Mortulak : Mortulak was the youngest and most blood-hungry child of Abaelat and Saeth. He was very muscular and strong and he rarely lost a fight. Much like his brother he loved seeing pain and suffering being inflicted upon mortals but even Gods too. He very often challenged other Gods and sometimes even lowered his power level on purpose in order to make the fights more interesting for him as he didn't like winning very easy. His power was equal to that of a Major God but he usually lowered his power levels on purpose to that of a Medium Deity.

Children of New Gods

Elpir – Eira → Evalion – Sephantil – Mystarin
Nechtan – Satkasi → Poseillia – Vantaur
Solton – Luminia → Eclipsi – Apol

Evalion : Evalion was the firstborn child of Elpir and Eira and unlike any other New God offspring, Evalion did not have a gender. Evalion was born genderless which was a rare sight, especially in God offspring's but that did not matter to Elpir and Eira as they raised Evalion as they would raise any of their other children and eventually they saw Evalion grow to become one of the highest regarded fighters among the Gods, only rivalled and ever defeated by Mortulak. Evalion's power was on the same level as that of a Major God.
Sephantil : Sephantil was the middle son of Elpir and Eira, a very skilled spell caster very well versed in the art of magic and especially in the healing arts that were passed down by his mother. Sephantil chose a life of solitude in order to research new spells and ways of healing without interruptions. He occasionally helped out travellers and animals that he found injured in his travels.
His powers were considered to be equal to those of a Major God.
Mystarin : Mystarin was the youngest daughter of Elpir and Eira, combining both her parents powers to a very big degree, Mystarin was considered to be a prodigy among the Children of the New Gods as her powers were equal to that of an Aspect and even some of the Aspects were slowly acknowledging her. She actively helped the mortal races and cared for the magical beings of the realm by becoming the Goddess of Magic.
Elpir, her father gladly gave the Domain of Magic to his daughter as she seemed to be surpassing even him in her proficiency in Magic. Thus, the Mistress of Magic, Mystarin was born as a Major God to rule over Magic along with her father.
Mystarin's powers were considered to be equal to those of an Aspect.

Poseillia : Poseillia was the eldest daughter of Satkasi and Nechtan, her beauty was unmatched by anything other than her strength in combat. After a petty squabble with Avernus and Mortulak, she was cursed by them never to walk the lands of mortal races again and they turned her legs into a fishtail. No matter how powerful she was, her power could not rival that of two Aspect offspring's and she was cursed to roam the oceans and never to walk on land again.
Vantaur : Vantaur was the youngest son of Nechtan and Satkasi, a very handsome young God with a gentle soul. He was so enraged when he learned what Avernus and Mortulak did to his dear sister that he vowed revenge against them and to find a way to free his sister from their curse.

Eclipsi : Eclipsi was the twin sister of Apol, very much like her father she loved the sunshine, light and the warmth that came with them but her powers bloomed under her mother's night sky and the soft light of the moon.
The children of Solton and Luminia strangely enough had not only the combined power of their parents but it seemed that their powers were on equal footing to that of an Aspect.
Apol : Apol was the twin brother of Eclipsi, much like his mother he loved the night, the darkness and the quiet that came with them but his powers bloomed under his Father's morning sky and the bright light of the sun.
The children of Solton and Luminia strangely enough had not only the combined power of their parents but it seemed that their powers were on equal footing to that of an Aspect.

Demi-Gods and other Divine Offspring's

Throughout the centuries there were a lot of Demi-Gods and other Divine offspring's that were spawned by the Gods but the only immortal ones were the ones that were born into divinity by both parents.
If a God had an offspring with any member of the mortal races, then that offspring might indeed have some of that Gods powers and might have had a somewhat expanded life-span but would not be immortal to aging or being killed by mortal weapons etc.

*Aval'es seemed very fond of his creations offspring's and tried to befriend them in their short lifespans to amuse himself even further. During his time among them, he grew close to some of them that he was very fond off. Some of them have been granted eternal life in a new plane of existence that only Aval'es had access to in order not to betray his existence to the rest of the Aspects and Deities he "faked" their deaths and sent them to his plane of existence.

Forms/Schools of Magic

Abjuration - Magical spells and effects within the school of abjuration are primarily designed for protection and shielding. Don't be fooled however, some Abjuration spells can pack quite a punch.
Abjuration "Protecting' stuff" (Abjure: to renounce)
They create magical barriers, negate harmful effects, harm trespassers, or banish creatures to other planes.

Conjuration - The School of Conjuration deals with creating objects and creatures or making them disappear.
Conjuration "Makin' stuff" (Conjure: to create)
Spells involve the transportation of objects and creatures from one location to another. Some spells summon creatures or objects to the caster's side, whereas others allow the caster to teleport to another location. Some conjurations create objects or effects out of nothing.

Evocation - Casters within the school of evocation unleash a raw magical energy upon their enemies. Whether it be flames, ice, or pure arcane energy: evocation spell casters are here to deal damage and chew gum... and they're all out of gum.
Evocation "Makin' energy stuff" (Evoke: cause an effect)
Spells manipulate magical energy to produce a desired effect. Some call up blasts of fire or lightning. Others channel positive energy to heal wounds.

Transmutation - Casters who study within the School of Transmutation are able to manipulate the physical properties of both items and people. This could be something simple – such as turning copper into gold – or could be an advanced spell that turns you into a newt (it'll get better...)
Transmutation "Changing' stuff" (Transmute: to change)
Spells change the properties of a creature, object, or environment. They might turn an enemy into a harmless creature, bolster the strength of an ally, make an object move at the caster's command, or enhance a creature's innate healing abilities to rapidly recover from injury.

Divination - The Magical School of Divination is centred around revealing and granting knowledge and information to the caster. Useful for reading ancient scripts, identifying magical items, and seeing invisible enemies.
Divination "Knowing' stuff" (Divine: discover or learn)
Spells reveal information.

Enchantment - Spells within the School of Enchantment are designed to manipulate the mental state of the target. This entire school is very similar to hypnotism, where the affected creature may act completely differently than how they normally behave.
Enchantment "Convincing' stuff" (Enchant: to cause someone to act in a way it usually wouldn't)
Spells affect the minds of others, influencing or controlling their behaviour.

Illusion - The School of Illusion is concerned with manipulating the various senses of people and creatures. This could be vision, hearing, or other various senses such as body temperature.
Illusion "Tricking' stuff" (Illusion: a deception)
Spells deceive the senses or minds of others.

Necromancy - In general, think of spells within the School of Necromancy as manipulating the ebb and flow of different creatures' "life energy", or the balance of energy between life and death. This can come across in the form of helping resurrection or draining necrotic damage.
Necromancy "Dead stuff" (Necro: death)
Spells manipulate the energies of life and death. Such spells can grant an extra reserve of life force, drain the life energy from another creature, create the undead, or even bring the dead back to life.

Breakdown of the Races:

Humans

The life expectancy of an average human is between 80 and 100 years old with some rare occasions that some reach the age of 120.
They come of age at the age of 18.

1 - Northern High

They are commonly referred to as barbarians since they live in tribal settlements in the freezing north, hunt for their sustenance, and are rarely seen in towns.
They are usually found in the Barbarian Capital of the North, Highguard.
Some of them have the ability to conduct magic, although it is typically their Seers and Shamans who do so.

2 – Omnitrelians

Omnitrel's inhabitants and those in the neighbouring areas. They are well-versed in magic and trade, and as a civilisation, they place a high priority on knowledge and prosperity.
They are the epitome of Omnia's Human civilisation.

3 – Levalents

the Humans of the Levalent Isles are known for being seafarers, traders, and travellers.
They prefer to sail the waters of Omnia despite having access to flying ships.
Their capital is Leval, which is located in the heart of the Levalent Isles.

4 - Slavers of Betlan Bay

The Slavers of Betlan Bay were initially a part of the High Northern barbarian tribes that came to the south a few centuries back and after pillaging around and living like "highwaymen" and were mainly based at the edge of the Great Desert at the Bay of Betlan. They realized they could make a fortune if they would capture and sell people from the villages and towns they've pillaged and sold them as slaves.

They The Slavers of Betlan Bay were born, a name that would strike fear into the hearts of mere villagers anywhere in the Omnitrellian continent.
They have a lot of main trade routes that supply them with goods and in exchange they provide slaves.
The High Elves of Kylles'ar, as well as the Demons of Wajun, are their principal trading partners, as both require a regular supply of slaves.
In exchange, the High Elves provide them with all of the necessary supplies to feed their people, while the Demons of Wajun equip them with lethal armament.

5 – Glaorvents

Glaorvents are residents of the Glaor area, a dark region with marshes and dark woodlands that few people venture

into.
Many Glaorvents are known to practise Dark & Blood Magic, which has been outlawed to the races of Omnia since ancient times by old laws and treaties signed by all races.

Humans and Magic

Humans are usually versed in **all** forms of magic in the world of Omnia but inherently proficient with abjuration and evocation magic.
Humans have in their nature to cause either great destruction or to protect.

Elves

The life expectancy of an average Elf is between 2500 and 3000 years old with some rare occasions that some reach the age of 3500.
They come of age at the age of 180.

1 - High Elves

Usually found at the top of Elven society as rulers. They live in Kylles'ar, the eastern Elven capital city.
They trade with all races, but Mermaids and Mermen are held in high regard because of their extraordinary thirst for knowledge.
Magic users with a high level of skill who can cast devastating spells.

2 - Dark Elves

They live underground and only interact with other races when absolutely necessary. Although they are as proficient in magic as the High Elves, it is said that some of them frequently use Dark and Blood Magic.

3 - Rogue Elves

The lowest class of elves, frequently utilised as slaves by the High Elves or on the front lines of battle because they are considered expendable. Because they were never taught how to utilise magic, just a few Rogue Elves know how to use it.

4 – Half-Elves

The life expectancy of an average Half-Elf is between 120 and 150 years old with some rare occasions that some reach the age of 200.
They come of age at the age of 18 as Humans do.

Because of the other half of their genealogy, they are never allowed to reside in Elven settlements because they are considered unclean blooded. Human, Dwarven, Gnomish, and even Harrim and Scultar cities are common places to

find them.
Although many Half-Elves can use magic and are competent at it, the majority of Half-Elves opt to follow the path of the healer, casting only healing magic.

Elves are well versed in all forms of magic. They favour Evocation, Illusion, Enchantment and Conjuration mostly.
Dark Elves very much like the Elves are also very well versed in all forms of magic. They favour Evocation, Illusion, Enchantment and Necromancy in their studies of magic.

Harrim & Scultar

The life expectancy of an average Harrim or Scultar is between 300 and 400 years old with some rare occasions that some reach the age of 500.
They come of age at the age of 80.

Harrim and Scultar are anthropomorphic creatures who live in the same manner as humans. The Harrim and Scultar are found all over the world, but their major capital is on the island of Scuhhart in the western part of the Levalent Isles.
They like hunting, fishing, and, on occasion, trading with foreign countries.
Scultar, on the other hand, are more animalistic in nature than Harrim.
As a result, Harrim is more likely to be the leader of their community, while Scultar is more likely to be the brawn.
The Harrim and Scultar used to have a war with the Mermen of Atalante over "**fishing**" disputes; Scultar would often fish near Mermen hunting grounds, which sparked a short war that lasted a little over 6 months and ended with them signing a treaty because everyone quickly realised that having a war would cost them a lot of money, so they instead formed an alliance with excellent trade relations and agreements for both sides.

The Harrim and Sculttar are somewhat versed in magic. Usually it's their Seers and Shamans that are versed in it and they favour Divination, Enchantment and Abjuration as their preferred schools of magic.

Gnomes

The life expectancy of an average Gnome is between 1100 and 1400 years old with some rare occasions that some reach the age of 1600.
They come of age at the age of 200.
Gnomes live in the serene city of Unispark to the west of Omnitrel. They are master craftsmen and engineers who collaborate closely with the Quessoc Mountain Dwarves to develop their magnificent marvels.
They have great magical abilities, but they prefer to use technology whenever feasible.

The Gnomes of Unispark are VERY well versed in all forms of magic, being the geniuses that they are that is to be expected. They favour Illusion, Evocation and Enchantment as their preferred schools of magic.

Dwarves

The life expectancy of an average Dwarf is between 1500 and 2000 years old with some rare occasions that some reach the age of 2500.
They come of age at the age of 250.

1 – Dwarves of Queattin.

The Quessoc Dwarves are a hardy bunch who live largely in Queattin, their capital city. They're outstanding miners and metallurgists, and even better weapon-smiths and armour-smiths. They have a strong bond with the Gnomes of Unispark, with whom they frequently collaborate to build magnificent creations.
They have a strong affinity for magic and frequently incorporate it into their weapons and armour in order to enhance it as much as possible. The Dwarves of Queattin invented some of the most powerful weapons in Omnia's history.

2 - Deep Dwarves

The Dark Dwarves live in the Deep End of the Quessoc Mountains, where they rarely see the sun. They have acclimated to the darkness and are skilled miners who frequently supply the Queattin Dwarves with rare minerals in return for food and other things.

The Quessoc Dwarves are decent spell casters who are versed in Abjuration, Divination, and Transmutation. The vast majority of them favour Transmutation as their preferred form of magic which helps them in everyday tasks and crafts.

Dragons

The life expectancy of an average Dragon is between 5000 and 7000 years old with some rare occasions that some reach the age of 9000.
They come of age at the age of 500.
In the world of Omnia, dragons are not what one might assume.
Even within their cities, they usually take human form, which is why they have them built to human height requirements.
Bahalen, their capital city, is a wealthy metropolis located above the Great Omnic Sea, typically between the Omnitrel and the Shan'at Desert. (We say usually because Bahalen is a flying city that follows the Dragons wherever they want it to go; it was once part of the Glaor region before it was corrupted.)
They are extremely powerful, having extraordinary wit and magic talents, yet they rarely employ it in battle.
A Dragon is supposed to be capable of annihilating mountains with a single spell if he unleashes all of his magical abilities for war.

The great race of the Dragons is gifted with great power over magic and can use all schools of magic with ease, they do not favour any one of them but abhor Necromancy.

Celestials

Celestials are an Immortal race that was created by the Gods as Guardians of Omnia and in order to fight at their Great Aspect War. They were cursed by Malekus to continue their never-ending Conflict so that he would continue to leech power through it.
Celestials are divine beings who live in the heavens in Omnia's realm. Their Silver City, which floats above the sky of the Shan'at Desert, serves as a guardian of the globe.
While still obeying the Gods, they have created a society and are led by the strongest of the Celestials, Lesyon the White, blessed by the Gods to lead the Celestials in the Eternal War against the Demons and titled “the redeemer”.
They have tremendous magical aptitude and destructive powers, similar to Dragons. They have been at odds with each other and the Demon race for thousands of years, ever since Malekus put the “**Curse of War**” on them.
The Celestials cannot reproduce as they were created by the Gods only for war but during the ages there have been testimonies of Celestials falling in love with mortals and having offspring's that could rival in power even the best warriors of their race.
These half-bloods are never seen as equal and are often left in the mortal world as they are not immortal as their Celestial parent and can die just like any mortal, their only benefit is bolstered strength and stamina and expanded lifespan.

The Celestials are blessed by the Gods to be able to use all schools of magic with ease but their favourite ones are Evocation and Abjuration.

Demons

Demons were once Celestials that were created by the gods and followed the God of War, Malekus. After the Great Aspect War lost to the Aspect of Death and got imprisoned, their appearance drastically changed they gained features such as yellow or red eyes, bat like wings, spikes coming out of various parts of their body, ever burning flames onto parts of their body etc.
The Demons of Omnia are horrible beings who after they changed, they withdrew to the city of in Wajun, which later came to be known as the Demonic City of Wajun, which is located in the world of Omnia's South-Eastern area, surrounded by mountains, volcanoes, the Had'Alet Mountains which is the battlefield the God fought during the Great

Aspect War and still has the craters of that battle, and monster-infested oceans.
After their horrific transformation, the Gods decided to exile them along with the whole city to another plane of existence with later came to be known as "**The Demonic Realm**". The entrance to it lies within the image of the once great city that was left where the city hovered over and it is said that a lot of Demons have found a way to come and go as they please.
They are led by one of the once strongest Celestials, now self-proclaimed Demon lord, Zephyr the Black. After transforming he left his old name and came to be known as Abaddon the Black.
They prefer mostly to seduce or try to corrupt other races whenever they have the chance in order to gather supporters for their unending war against the rest of the Celestials as their one true goal is to free their lord, Malekus.
Unfortunately the Demonic race cannot reproduce in order to create new Demons but they have found that they can affect the mortal races and by seducing them they can create half-demonic beings that sometimes are quite powerful to rival the Celestials on their own and thus this is the course they've taken in order to bolster their numbers.
Their offspring's are often being offered to be taken and trained in the Demonic City of Wajun where they will learn and fight alongside them against the Celestials. They are often welcome with open arms as they benefit from bolstered strength and stamina and while they are not immortal like their parents and can die like any mortal, they have somewhat expanded lifespan.

Very much like the Celestials, Demons can use all schools of magic but they favour Evocation and Necromancy most of all.

Mermaid / Merman

The life expectancy of an average Mermaid or Merman is between 500 and 700 years old with some rare occasions that some reach the age of 900.
They come of age at the age of 50.
The Mermaids and Mermen of the Underwater Kingdom of Atalante are proud and attractive beings that reside in their underwater city near Eastern border of the Levalent Isles.
They have a strong affinity for magic and are willing to share their knowledge with other species in exchange for the same amount of knowledge, as they place a great value on knowledge and information.
They've evolved and invented a number of underwater spells to keep them safe from various aquatic monsters.
They used to have a war with the Harrim and Scultar over hunting issues, which lasted only 6 months. However, both sides quickly realised that fighting would cost them far more, so they formed a powerful alliance with mutually advantageous trading links.

The race of Mermen / Mermaids is blessed with a high ability to produce and control magic. They have great magical powers but tend not to use them as often as the other races of Omnia, when they do they do produce wonders. Their most favoured schools of magic are Abjuration, Conjuration, Divination, Transmutation and Illusion

NOTABLE PLACES

Omnitrel - The Omnitrelians' Capital City serves as the principal bulwark of humanity in Omnia. Omnitrel's market, the main centre of trade for Omnia's human population, is claimed to have just about everything because it has been trading with all regions of the planet for millennia.

The Frozen North - Highguard - The Quessoc Mountains are home to the wandering tribes of the High Northern and the Quessoc Dwarves. Trading is limited in the freezing north, and only a few travelling merchants may be seen roving the roads from tribe village to tribe village. A big caravan supplying Omnitrel & Kylles'ar passes through its main roadways every few weeks making its way to the Northern Capital of Highguard that is the stop for every tribe willing to trade goods in the North.

Levalent Isles - The Levalent Isles, which consist of 200 islands and are centred on the largest island, Leval, are the largest cluster of Isles in the globe of Omnia.
As expected, Leval is the Isles' commerce centre, bringing together unusual items from all across Omnia, including Omnitrel, Kylles'ar, Scuhhart, Unispark, Queattin, Bahalen, and the Underwater Kingdom of Atalante.

Glaorean Swamps - The Glaorean Swamps are located beyond the Great Omnic Sea to the south, and they cover the majority of the Glaor region, leaving Dark and Haunted forests in their wake. The Demons of Wajun corrupted a lot of the high mages of Doradel and the whole region fell to their corruption.
Doradel was a human metropolis that had long been lost inside the region's Dark and Haunted woodlands and Dark Swamps. It is supposed to be home to some of Omnia's most ferocious and terrifying beasts and creatures.
There is no trade in the Glaor region, and traders are rarely seen unless they have been disoriented.

Kylles'ar - Kylles'ar is the High Elves' major and capital city. Kylles'ar's marketplace is their civilization's main commerce centre, and you could claim that you can find just about everything there, including items that are even more exotic than those found in Omnitrel.

Scuhhart - The proud Harrim and Scultar city of Scuhhart is on the border of the Chatt'un Desert, in an oasis-like environment where the land meets the sea. Scuhhart was originally only a little port city, but as its final inhabitants went to seek a better life at Unispark or Omnitrel, the Harrim and Scultar came in, and over the years, they constructed something truly magnificent, the city of Scuhhart, which is a mixture of their names.
Both Omnitrel and the Underwater Kingdom of Atalante have a health trade with Scuhhart.

Unispark - Others think the Gnomes of Unispark are an odd bunch. They are, without a doubt, geniuses of the first order. Even the most brilliant Elven Wizards could not conceive what it would take to successfully combine magic and technology to the degree that they have.
The Gnomes created their home just south-east of the Quessoc Mountain range, in the mountains of Unisat, by combining old and abandoned Dwarven mines used to extract Omnium Crystals.
They were fleeing their ancient habitat in the Glaor region due to the corruption and damage brought about by the Celestial-Demon war, and they eventually found sanctuary in the abandoned Dwarven mines, which they decided to call home.
They made the best of the mines, made friends with the Quessoc Dwarves, who offered the Gnomes assistance in establishing their new homeland, and finally not only did they build it, but Unispark now stands as one of the only entirely magical-technological cities in all of Omnia.
The Gnomes of Unispark owe a great debt to the Dwarves of Quessoc, not only for assisting them in establishing their new kingdom, but also for allowing them to exploit their old mines, which they practically still owned.
After Unispark was established and the Gnomes finally had a home, they felt very indebted to the Dwarves and requested that they send a convoy of their brightest scientists to confer with the Dwarves on how and if they could help improve their own capital as the least they could to thank them, which the Dwarves gladly agreed to.
As a result, the Queark Cannons and the Dome of Preservation of Queattin, two of Omnia's strongest defences, were built.
Unispark has numerous trade agreements with a variety of races, the majority of them are with Queattin.

Quessoc Mountains (Queattin) - Queattin is the Dwarven Kingdom's capital, situated in the heart of the Quessoc Mountains. The Dwarves spend their days mining Omnium Crystals and other resources from their mines, which they then trade or utilise to construct amazing things. Except for the Gnomes of Unispark, with whom they have a wonderful relationship, they have little interaction with the world outside the Quessoc Mountains.
Queattin's capital city is also guarded by Omnia's strongest defences, the Queark Cannons and the Dome of Preservation, which were built by a partnership of Gnomes and Dwarves.
The Queark Cannons are claimed to be capable of decimating hundreds of troops with a single shot, and the Gnomes have made these cannons fire six times in ten seconds. The Dome of Preservation, on the other hand, is a magical shield fuelled by a large number of Omnium Crystals that protects a 2 kilometre radius around Queattin's capital city, preventing both magical and non-magical missiles from being fired.
While the Dwarves dislike dealing with strangers, they do have a large number of merchants that come to their capital to buy their commodities (armour, weapons, and marvellous items) and sell them other materials or food.

Bahalen - Bahalen is the Dragons' Great Flying City.
Bahalen was originally located in the northern part of Omnia, directly above the Glaorean region, but after the Glaorean region became corrupted during the Great Celestial-Demon war, the Dragon Council of Bahalen decided that it would be best for all of their citizens to relocate the city to the northern border of Omnitrel.
Bahalen is mainly self-sufficient, as dragons, being old beings, prefer not to rely on other races and prefer to remain alone.
They rarely interfere in mortal concerns, but they do maintain a watchful eye on what happens in Omnia.
Omnitrel, Queattin, Unispark, The Underwater Kingdom of Atalante, and even Scuhhart have trading agreements with

them.

The Silver City - All Celestial beings of Omnia call the Great Proud Silver City home. Celestials are divine beings created by the gods to protect Omnia's world before they created the other species.
They've been at odds with the Demons for thousands of years, dating back to when the Gods founded Omnia and before the fall of Malekus when the Demons were still very much like them, Celestials.
The Gods retired to their divine domain and transported the great Silver City along with them.
Some mortal cities and territories were caught in its aftermath during the Great War, leaving death, ruin, and in some cases lasting taint in the world, as Demons are known to do.
The Celestials never interfere in mortal matters and have no desire for trade because they are self-sufficient and do not require food or water.
They also build their own weapons out of Light Magic, Omnium, and small shards of their soul, making them unbreakable and lethal.

Demonic City of Wajun - The Ruined City of Wajun was once a mighty Elven colony that succumbed to Demons and the Demon Lord Abaddon's depravity.
It was simple for him to gradually transform the city into what it is now, a flaming hole of grief, lunacy, and debauchery suited only for Demons and Lost Souls, once he had grabbed control of the ruler's mind.
Abaddon, the Demon Lord, governs over all of Wajun and trains his Demons to fight the Celestials in the Great War.
Even though Demons, like Celestials, have no need for trade, they do have "understandings" with some shady characters in order to have a steady influx of slaves and damned souls that they need for sacrifices, to infuse in their spells, or even to use their souls to empower their weapons and make them devastating and indestructible.
Also, it is very common to see half-breeds wandering the streets of Wajun as they too help in the "**Eternal War**" as a considerable fighting force.
Much like the Celestials, the Demons create their own weapons but they use Dark Magic (instead of Light Magic as their transformation has corrupted them and they cannot use Light Magic anymore), Omnium and instead of using a small part of their soul like the Celestials do, they use slave souls that they get usually from the Slavers of Betlan Bay.

Underwater Kingdom of Atalante - Even though it is underwater, the Underwater Kingdom of Atalante is one of Omnia's most gorgeous kingdoms.
Once within, everyone is struck by how vibrant the sea's depths can be, as well as how inviting they are.
The Kingdom of Atalante is a true jewel in the oceans of Omnia, with natural illumination from the extraordinarily bright Omnium Crystals of the depths.
Atalante is situated in the heart of Omnia's oceans, surrounded by the Levalent Isles, different Sea Monsters, Sea Serpents, and the Kraken, the Guardian of its Gates.
The king was successful in establishing trading relationships with all races and kingdoms, ensuring their prosperity.

Magical Creatures : *Pegasus, Gryphon, Basilisk, Ghoul, Imp, Kelpie, Yeti, Hydra, Tarasque, Naga, Gorgon, Minotaur, Vampire, Werewolf, Ghost, Elemental, Ifrit, Hell-hound, Celestial, Demon, Cyclops, Valkyrie, Gargoyle, Nymph, Goblin, Troll, Ghoul, Skeleton, Satyr, Unicorn, Manticore, Fairy, Hippogriff, Sea Serpent, Sea Monster, Water Dragon, Hippocamp, Will-o'-the-wisp, Wendigo, Banshee, Cerberus, Earth Dragon, Hekantonkheires, Azure Dragon, Black Tortoise, Centaur, Spirit, Lich, Wraith, Undead, Djinn (Genie).*

Notable Large & Strong Magical Creatures: *Dragons, Stygia, Tarasque, Sea Dragon, Sea Serpent, Sea Monster, Leviathan, Kraken, Phoenix.*

NOTABLE ORGANIZATIONS

The Church of the 12: Considered to be one of the biggest organizations in the world of Omnia, The Church of the 12 is a religious organization with churches and branches all over the world. They worship and serve the 11 original Deities and while they do accept Malekus as one of the 12 original Deities, the worship for him has been forbidden ever since his imprisonment. They do not condone the worship of the new deities as they see them as lesser entities that are not worthy of worship. They have a special division within their organization for hunting down individuals with Malekus' Crimson Power and imprisoning them or putting them down.

The New God Order: They are a widely known organization that was founded about a millennia ago and is focused on worshiping the new deities. They do not mind worship of the Greater old deities but they kind of see them as ancient beings that do not care about the mortal races like the new Gods do.

The Purple Omni-Crusaders: They are the Elite fighting force of Omnitrel, they started off as a branch of the Omnitrellian army but soon broke off and started offering their services directly to the King. The King's guard is made entirely of Purple Omni-Crusaders and they are said to be the toughest and strongest humans to have ever lived. They go through rigorous training that only the best and brightest of the human race can endure.

The Blades of Yao'tal: The Blades of Yao'tal originate somewhere between myth and legend, they are said to be legendary warriors that help the weak and always appear in times of great distress. There are not many accounts of witnessing the Blades of Yao'tal but if the rumours are to be believed, they are one of the biggest organizations in the world of Omnia with ties to every aspect of every type of government and authority figure and they are ghosts that perform their actions within shadows. They gained their name from an old story that is passed from generation to generation within every race of Omnia, the story says that there once was an Elven King that saw a nymph in a forest and decided to make her his bride. He sent his emissary into the forest and after the nymph refused, he was so mad that he ordered his troops to slay every living thing within the forest.

The forest was the forest of Yao'tal or as it is now called "Eryn Vanimeld'a".

The forest's creatures and residents did not take well to the Kings order of slaying all living beings and they banded together to create the Blades of Yao'tal. Legend has it that they descended upon his soldiers from the shadows slaying everyone with their distinctive long blades before making their way to the Elven Capital to confront the King.

After slaying everyone in their path and reaching the throne room, the nymph that the King desired is said to have come forward and lowered her hood before driving her long blade through the King's heart and whispered "The Blades of Yao'tal will not rest while there are hearts as corrupt as yours in the world, we will always be here to end tyranny."

And thus the Legend of The Blades of Yao'tal was born, is there truth to the legend? Who's to say? Maybe, maybe not.

The 7 Archmages of Kylles'ar: The 7 Legendary Archmages of Kylles'ar is a council compromised of 7 Elves, all heads of the 7 noble families of Kylles'ar that possess immense power and knowledge of the arcane. Each of the 7 Elven Lords are very well versed in all forms of magic but specialised in 1 in particular, everyone has their own specialty and that is what makes The 7 Archmages terrifying.

Their command of magic cannot be rivalled in the world of Omnia. They often tend to stay away from matters of politics or war and their goal is to satisfy their never-ending hunger for knowledge about magic. It is said that Elpir, the God of magic came into existence just because the 7 Archmages believed he existed and wanted to "meet" him in order to gain more knowledge of magic.

The Phantoms of Glaor: The Phantoms of Glaor is said to be undead assassins that utilize their skills to perform assassinations throughout the continents of Omnia. A certain necromancy spell is required in order to summon them and their fee is usually either counted in souls or whatever the most prized possession of the summoner is. Their ranks are rumoured to be compromised by wraiths, vampires, ghosts and a lot more undead creatures. Usually one can find more information about them and their services within black markets that operate in every region under the authorities noses.

Currency

Humans : Omnitrelian coins (Copper, Silver, Gold, Platinum), Gems, Jopi (Universal Currency)
Elves : Kyless'ar coins (Copper, Silver, Gold, Platinum), Gems, Jopi (Universal Currency)
Dwarves : Queattin coins (Copper, Silver, Gold, Platinum), Gems, Jopi (Universal Currency)
Harrim & Scultar : Fish & Services, Harrim coins (Copper, Silver, Gold, Platinum), Gems, Jopi (Universal Currency)
Dragons : Gems, Jopi (Universal Currency)
Celestials : Daeva coins (Copper, Silver, Gold, Platinum), Gems, Jopi (Universal Currency)
Demons : Soul coins (coins that contain souls), Gems, Jopi (Universal Currency)

CHAPTER ONE - THE FATED CRASH

This is the storey of Omnia, a realm where legends and myths collide.
A realm filled with wonders, magic, and extraordinary animals, as well as a diverse range of races that live and thrive there. It is a world where everything is connected, from the air, to the water, the land, even the stars and planets.

Our storey begins with a young girl named Andremi. Although she is simply our hero's mother, you will see why our storey begins with her and her tragedy.
Andremi was the daughter of a wealthy ship captain, but not the kind you think of when you hear the word "ship," but a flying ship!
The mages of Omnia have managed to fuse magic and technology and create wondrous vehicles and everyday appliances that use magic as a power source through an Omnium crystal, thanks to the advancement of magic and technology hand in hand and the rare mineral Omnium, which is used as a magical power source due to its high concentration of magic.
So, Gaioz the First, Andremi's father, was a rather affluent merchant ship captain who frequently travelled the world of Omnia, exchanging products with its many races.
Chrissantel, Andremi's mother used to work in the world's largest tobacco plant in Omnitrel, the human continent's capital.
They decided that she should stay at home and raise their two children, Marialus and Andremi, after their marriage and her pregnancy.
Marialus, Andremi's brother, was always a hard-working young man, and despite the fact that his father had a business ready for him to take over, he desired more, so he enlisted in the army to seek adventure and excitement.
In Omnitrel, mandatory army service was usually reserved for poor villagers and people on the verge of poverty; they were given the option to join the army, receive magical training, and serve their country to the best of their abilities while being handsomely compensated, allowing their families to escape poverty.
Despite the fact that Marialus had no financial difficulties, he believed it was in his best interests to serve his country, which he did.
His love of the country and fellow soldiers, as well as his desire to prove that he could stand on his own, propelled him quickly through the ranks of the army and eventually drew him to a competition offered to the best of the best in the military in Omnitrel.
Each participant was given a magical sword and uniform, as well as a small army of soldiers to aid them in the battles.
Many of the soldiers in the crowd had never fought in a full-fledged battle before, so they were nervous.
His initial reservations were dispelled when he had an especially exciting fight in the competition with soldiers from Jodia and Vittorio and was complimented by the army's General for his sword mastery and hand-to-hand combat style.

Andremi, on the other hand, had no such ambitions; she was a dedicated learner, and a talented one at that, having mastered the five fundamental principles of magic at the tender age of six. She was a prodigy unlike any other, and by the age of 15, she had secured a scholarship to study under the Grand Meister, the King's most trusted advisor in matters of magic.
She was so ecstatic that when some of her friends invited her to join them in celebrating, she said yes without hesitation, and that's when things took a turn, and one seemingly innocuous decision would affect the fate of Omnia for millennia to come.
She went out with her friends in one of their magical carriages, and one of them suggested using a speeding spell to see how fast they could go. He did so, and after casting a spell to overcharge the carriage's Omnium crystal, giving it a huge boost of speed, they realised they couldn't control the flying vehicle.
This would drive them to fly uncontrollably around Omnitrel's crowded city until they collided with an abandoned warehouse.
The force of the crash was so severe that three of the five passengers were killed instantly, or so everyone assumed.
The city's security force dispatched Omnitrel Healers and Mages along with the City Guard to the warehouse to observe the devastating impact. Vasel, a friend of Andremi's, had her head chopped off as a result of the hit, and everyone else, including Andremi, was either on the verge of death or proclaimed dead on the spot; Andremi was one of the persons pronounced dead.
They'll return the dead to the Healer's Headquarters once they've cleansed the site.
Andremi was wrapped in a white sheet, waiting for her parents to receive the body for the funeral, when one of the young healers observed her raising her hand.

He quickly alerted the Grand Meister, who approached the body with two of the more experienced magicians to see if she was still alive or had been converted into an undead, a process they hadn't seen in at least three centuries.
When they discovered she wasn't undead and had been mysteriously revived, they took her to the hospital and used every healing spell they could think of, as well as healing potions and therapies, to restore her to full health.
Everything seemed to be going well, and her body would return to normal in a few months, but the Grand Meister was worried that her mind would never be the same.
Andremi had completely lost her ability to use magic for some reason, and she couldn't even do the most basic tasks with it.
There had never been anyone in recent history who had entirely lost their power, not while he was Grand Meister anyway; there had been reports of spell casters having their magic sealed, but she had none. On the other hand, no one has ever come back from the dead like she did without becoming an undead.
Andremi would undergo some intense treatments and examinations in the coming months, and she appeared to be doing fine at the end of them.
However, most of those treatments were very expensive, and her father had to sell most of their wealth to pay for them, leaving Andremi's brother bitter because he had everything he gained in the army to help out his family.

CHAPTER TWO - THE FAMILY

After some time, the increasingly middle-class (financially) family found a suitable lad, Jonah, a great shipwright, to marry Andremi.
Someone might believe that this is Andremi's happy ending, but they may be disappointed. There was no happy ending in this storey.
Andremi would eventually be pregnant, with twins no less. Both Andremi and Jonah were overjoyed and couldn't wait for their little angels to be born. Their joy would not last long as the fateful time of birth eventually drew closer and came. Andremi would be in labour for hours with Jonah pacing up and down the corridor while waiting. As the time drew closer Andremi blacked out and witnessed in her mind a dark figure. This Dark figure would be the spitting image of what she heard the Avatar of Demiur would look like, a cloaked and hooded figure that no one could see the face, carrying a scythe, very much like our own Grim Reaper.
The terrifying figure raised its skeletal hand and pointed forward towards Andremi's belly.
She felt as if something was pulling her from within and towards that strange figure; could it be that he wanted her children's souls? Even before they were born? She tried to resist but couldn't, so she burst into tears and begged uncontrollably.
She eventually saw a faint image of a baby being pulled out of her belly, and her grief and sadness were so overwhelming that she felt like dying, but at that moment, a second faint baby hand extended from her belly, seemingly grasping the image of the baby that was being pulled and pulling it back, this went on for a few seconds, and as the Avatar saw that he was being pushed back, he made a fist and tried to pull harder.
While Andremi was crying and pleading for the lives of her unborn children, she noticed a frail old man with an eye-patch on his left eye, standing beside her, calmly watching everything that was going on. As this unfolded, she noticed him raising his hand and a burst of Crimson Light forming a barrier in front of her, the image of her baby being pushed back into her belly while the barrier smashed that skeletal figure into smithereens like it disintegrated it, and a warm light filling her belly. She nodded to the old man, grateful that he had saved her. The old man seemed surprised, as if he hadn't expected her to thank him for some reason, and he raised his hand again, pointing to Andremi, filling her with a warm light that penetrated deep into her soul.
When Andremi regained consciousness and felt the pains of childbirth again, she tried to push with all the strength she had left, and her babies were born. Unfortunately, one of them died in childbirth; her baby girl, Christa, did not survive.
Was that a real vision? Did a Godly Avatar really try to murder her children when they were born?
Her baby boy was born, and unlike his unfortunate sister, he seemed to be in good health.

"- Gaioz!" Andremi said, "Your name shall be Gaioz," named after her late father, while she sobbed for her little girl.

Unfortunately, shortly after their son's birth, Jonah was injured in an accident while working on the construction of the King's new flying vessel, the vehicle frame fell on him, paralysing him. He was able to walk again after being tended by the Citadel's best Healers, but he would need a cane for the rest of his life.
Andremi's position did not improve either; she was still unable to use magic, and she was having nightmares and feeling her mind slipping away at times. She started saying that the God of Death was after her children and that he was the one that took Christa. No one would believe her when she told the story of Gaioz's birth and the strange old man that she saw, everyone thought she was completely losing her mind. Even Jonah couldn't say for sure if she was really losing her mind or not, after consulting with the Grand Meister who knew her situation and was the one who treated her, he was convinced of one thing. It will only get worse as she grew older.

NOTE - WHAT ACTUALLY HAPPENED -

Of course, we've always known what was going on with her.
When a soul crosses over to the next world, they are greeted by a massive gate. Everything that has ever happened, is occurring, or will ever happen somewhere in the myriad of worlds is hidden behind this barrier, much like **Aval'es** ability of seeing into the past, present and future at all times.

Andremi crossed over, stood on the threshold of this gate, stared into the abyss at past, present, and future, and, as they say, if you stare into the abyss long enough, the abyss will look back.
This was the Great Gate, through which souls passed when they crossed the threshold of this world and were ready to be judged in the Gods' realm.
Andremi couldn't cross the threshold because she wasn't completely dead nor had any Divine powers & abilities, she was just an ordinary mortal.
Malekus, the God who returned her gaze from his cage, chose her because of her strong will and deposited a seed in her. A seed that if she ever had children, they would be his children, the ones who would be able to free him from the enslavement of the other Gods.
This God was Malekus, the God of War.
When the "**Curse of Malekus**" was placed on Andremi, any children she bore would be his, and because she was about to have twins as witnessed at the Soul Gate when she was looking at her future, a boy and a girl, the "**Curse of Malekus**" would activate and empower these children with his power.
So, after seeing into Andremi's soul and inflicting the "**Curse of Malekus**" on her, she would return to the world of the living, but at the expense of her magic, which would be used to raise and strengthen his heirs, as was the case with everyone who received such a power.
Malekus also realised that seeing into the past, present, and future at the same time could destabilise and drive a delicate human mind insane, if not instantly, but because she was his chosen one, he would not let her go insane until she gave birth to his heirs.
He decided to use a large portion of his power to create a barrier in Andremi's mind. Andremi was fortunate in that she was not driven insane immediately, but rather gradually lost what little sanity she had over time.
However, when she was giving birth, Demiur's Avatar, the Avatar of Death, sensed something very unnatural being brought into the realm of Omnia and rushed to see what it could be.
Much to his surprise, he witnessed a human giving birth to 2 children that had the power of a **God**. He had encountered similar situations before as he knew that his brother was trying to plan his escape but he never thought that he would witness the birth of new deities, from a human no less.
After witnessing this, the Avatar decided it was best to exterminate the twins before they would actually be born in the world, because he could sense Malekus' power within them. Fortunately for our hero, the Avatar of Death was not the only one who sensed this; **Aval'es** also teleported as soon as he sensed this power coming to the world and he was also present, invisible to the Avatar's eyes, only visible to the children's souls as he didn't worry because he knew the "**Catharsis**" souls go through, would make them forget about him.
He decided to let one of the children live and fused the soul of the other within it, giving it even more power.
He significantly increased the power Malekus bestowed on Andremi, allowing the Avatar of Death to be pushed back without leaving any traces of his involvement. It was then that he felt pity on the innocent soul that lost its chance to life cause of the Avatar of Death, his creation. He extended his hand and an intense electric blue ball appeared, he then proceeded to infuse that ball with Christa & Gaioz and a soft, soothing but bass voice sounded saying:

"- I'm sorry younglings, no fleeting mortal soul should have to go through what you went through, I have decided, I am going to bestow my protection upon you and also I'm going to give you a gift so that one day you may decide what you want for yourselves and entertain this old man a little more."

By infusing this bright blue ball with the souls of Andremi's children, he gave them part of his power, the part that he had ripped out, his ability to see the future along with some other protections and gifts to shield them from the Gods while they live their short mortal lives.

After all, this was all for his entertainment; it wouldn't be as much fun if the Divine beings knew he was involved.

Christa's soul was joined with Gaioz, leaving him with a distinct intense electric blue coloured left eye and the ability to see his sister's ghost since birth, as well as use her Crimson Barriers powers.

He was also blessed by **Aval'es**, who bestowed a powerful protection on the children souls, ensuring that Divine beings would never be able to track them down or claim their souls again, making their souls immortal.

Andremi, who was witnessing all of this, surprisingly understood what the stranger was doing, despite the fact that it was unlike any magic she had ever seen in her life; she nodded gratefully to the stranger because she could only see **Aval'es** in his human form, as a frail old man, which surprised even **Aval'es** himself, a mortal who could see him without his permission? A mortal that understood what he did?

He was impressed and a little bit confused but most of all, very entertained by the whole situation, he wished at times like these that he could see the future but instantly dismissed the thought as it would not be as entertaining. He decided to protect her as well, and with a single swift hand gesture, he made her soul immortal, and when she'd died, she would join him as a Divine being.

He vanished shortly after the hand gesture, and Andremi assumed she was having a strange dream or nightmare.

Now, let's get back to the present...

CHAPTER THREE - TOUGH CHILDHOOD -

Jonah and Andremi were being very overprotective of Gaioz Jr during the first years of his life, having lost their stillborn daughter Christa and Andremi still remembering the hooded figure and the old man that saved her. They went out of their way to make him feel very loved and cared for though.

Gaioz could always see a little girl right next to him as a baby, a little girl that seemed to be growing up alongside him. The curious thing was that no one else was able to see her and when Gaioz asked his mother about it, she burst into tears and said that this is certainly the soul of his late twin sister that was born dead alongside him, she was convinced that somehow the soul of her little girl was following Gaioz in his life, growing beside him and was both happy and sad about that fact.

In his early years, Gaioz was a model student with a firm command of magic, just like his mother had been when he was his age, a prodigy in the making. Other kids had firm control over one or two magical elements while Gaioz seemed to have perfect control over all of them.

Unfortunately, he was unable to concentrate on his studies as well as his mother. He had a lot of obligations and a lot on his mind, despite his youth.

At the same time, Gaioz felt compelled to look after his parents as he grew older, observing his father struggle after his accident and his mother slowly losing her mind over time.

He would sometimes put his education on hold in order to care for his family. He was a quiet and gentle young man with a large circle of friends, even though that he was bullied a lot as a child due to the unnatural intense colour of his left eye.

Gaioz's generosity and good disposition transformed at some time in his childhood, around the age of seven. A "friend" of his, a boy 5 years older than him, duped him and cornered him one day, and that sick, sneaky and perverted kid eventually would molest him.

Gaioz felt he couldn't turn to anyone for support growing up in a family like his. That would continue for another two years, the pain of that act haunting him, and when he considered starting a family of his own, he would reflect on what had happened to him and worry if he could ever have a regular life and family.

Despite this, Gaioz would persevere in his life by having little to no faith in people, playing scenarios and imagining the outcomes of any event he encountered 10,000 times in his thoughts, identifying all the negative possibilities and focusing on avoiding them. In interacting with the rest of the world, that was his coping method.

He developed a VERY defensive magic style, an impenetrable shell that not even his instructors could penetrate, and everyone felt he was a true prodigy.

The truth is that he created this type of magic subconsciously in order to protect himself, his mother, and anyone else

he cared about from the cruelty of the world, which he discovered early in life.
At this point, he would occasionally begin to hear voices, which he ignored at first but became more intense over time, prompting him to investigate. He went on to decipher entire books on the subject of hearing voices and what they could be or mean, as it could be a variety of things. He came across a text in an old book about soul binding after ruling out Gods, Ghosts, and any other supernatural beings he could find in the books.
Soul Binding was a type of magic that bound one or more souls together. It was most commonly used to bind the soul of a great person to continue helping the living with a task that he was great at while alive. For example, binding a great general's soul in order to help his countrymen continue a war with his great strategic mind. As Necromancy became a taboo, Soul Binding was quickly outlawed.
The act of binding two or more souls together and hearing them when they cried out. He immediately turned to look at the girl who was always looking over his shoulder; oddly, he hadn't paid attention to her since he was molested. He noticed her sobbing uncontrollably and yelling at the top of her lungs, but all Gaioz could hear was a muffled whisper. He rushed and dug his face into the book, reading more about soul binding and how someone could hear a soul that was bound to him because he was too certain that this was the soul of his late twin sister, as his mother had told him all these years ago.
He eventually discovered a spell that allowed him to interact with her and even have normal conversations with her. The only problem was that this spell was a Necromancy spell, a school of magic that had been banned from the world of Omnia centuries ago, but that would not deter him; he would cast that spell no matter what. He dashed off to gather all of the materials for the spell and began the chant.
A black force of death energy and black cracking lightning burst through the signs he had drawn on the ground, and a black light emanated from the ghostly girl beside him, making her image clearer. As the light faded, they stood looking at each other as clear as day, and she went forward and hugged her brother, exclaiming:

- "At long last! I can hug my younger brother! I'm sorry you had to go through everything without being able to speak to anyone, but I'm here now! Thank you very much, little brother!"

They were both overjoyed and sat there for hours talking. Finally, Gaioz appeared to have someone with whom he could converse and confide in. He considered telling his mother about Christa, but after discussing it with his sister, they decided to keep quiet for fear of aggravating her condition, so they agreed to remain silent on the matter.
Eventually, the siblings discovered new ways to collaborate that they could never have imagined, including the creation of new spells and much more. Furthermore, Christa told him about what happened during their birth and confirmed their mother's claims of a skeletal hooded figure attacking her in a dream and a frail old man assisting her. She was able to retain these "**memories**" because her soul did not experience the same "**Catharsis**" that every soul experiences when they are born into the world.
The Gods have an odd sense of irony in that they allow souls to retain all of their memories of previous lives until they are brought into this world by another being. That is when the "**Catharsis**" occurs, an ancient spell created by Leandra and Demiur that erases any memories of previous lives, allowing it to begin anew in its new life.
With all of this previously unknown information, Gaioz went forward in life with a new resolve and purpose, to find a way to "**mend**" his mother's broken mind, even if it meant going against the Gods themselves (which he had no idea he would) and find out why the God of Death had targeted him and his sister even before they were born.
He continued his studies as he grew older and into a teenager, and he was even one of the top students in his class in every subject, including Magic, Math, Strategy, and Finance. There was nothing he couldn't accomplish.
He was gifted a brand new Omni-bike by his grandmother shortly after receiving his Academy grades, as he had been begging his parents to get him one, a single-person vehicle that was popular among young people at the time.
This bike, which was powered solely by an Omnium crystal and a moderate anti-gravity spell, could soar through the sky at incredible speeds and was very popular among Omnitrel's young people looking for a buzz.
Unfortunately, as soon as Gaioz got his Omni-bike, he started skipping classes to spend time with friends who also had Omni-bikes, and they would fly around aimlessly, going for long rides around the villages of Omnitrel, feeling completely free. After feeling trapped with taking care of his family for so long, he seemed to long for a sense of freedom and saw this as an opportunity to escape for a short time.
Christa remained silent because she knew what her brother had gone through in his life and wanted him to have this chance at happiness, even if it was only for a short time.
His academic performance gradually deteriorated, but it wasn't long before things went from bad to worse.
Gaioz's first relationship began when he was 15 years old, with a girl named Dorael.
He was dating a girl two years his senior at the time.
Gaioz gave his entire attention and energy to his new romance, putting his friends and studies on hold. It was the first time in his life that he had felt anything like this. At the same time, he began working as an assistant in a local store.

That's when he started to become a little more streetwise, and he added that to his already brilliant mind.
Gaioz and Dorael were together for about four years before she broke his heart and moved on with someone much older than both of them. Gaioz's dreams were shattered in an instant, and all his hopes for a future with Dorael vanished when he went to pick her up one day and saw her getting into another man's vehicle. He attempted to confront Dorael to find out what was going on because he didn't want to believe it at first, but she refused to even speak to him.
Life was proving to Gaioz once more that it isn't always fair and can be harsh, even in matters of love.

CHAPTER 4 - ALL OUT WAR

Soon after his heart was broken, war had come to Omnitrel, two years before his graduation from the Magic Academy, and Gaioz would learn how harsh life could be.
A war with the elves in the east had been brewing for years, and now, following a new "**misunderstanding**" war was about to break out.
Within the next 5 years, and all able-bodied magical users were drafted into the army, as they would need to push back the Elven invaders and hopefully push them even further than where they came from to take a piece of their lands as well.
As a result, Gaioz was drafted into the army with almost nothing left for him back home.
His mother divorced his father when he was ten years old, his father died of a heart condition when he was fifteen, and his grandfather died when he was three, leaving him to be raised by a "**unstable**" Andremi and his loving grandmother.
He had to travel to the country's border in the forests of the T'Lanth region, near the Shim'Lar Lakes, after being enlisted in the army, where the army of Omnitrel would meet the Elven forces of Kylles'ar.
He was supposed to report to Captain Zorad on the front lines to find out where he was going to be deployed.
He narrowly avoided a barrage of fireball spells aimed at the vehicles that transported him and many others to the front lines after arriving and witnessing the first of the battles at the border, but others were not so lucky. As he rushed out of his transport vehicle, he saw the battlefield burning after the barrage of fireballs hit; many men lay dead, while others tried to extinguish the fires on people and equipment alike.
Only 23 of the 180 troops transferred in the convoy Gaioz was a part of survived.
The Elves appeared to want to end the war before it even started by attacking supply and troop carriers.
As soon as the supply and troop vehicles exploded, a flood of spells descended from the sky, as the elves refused to give up pressing forward with more tenacity in their barrage of spells.
After witnessing their cruelty, Gaioz was so enraged by the death and destruction around him, as well as the belittlement of the human lives being wasted, but before he could think or act, a new barrage of fireball and acid rain spells were launched upon the surviving soldiers in his area. He froze in time, he didn't have time to think or act as Christa appeared right next to him, extending her arms towards the spells and shouted:

"- Brother, do as I do! We can stop them and save everyone!"

Without a moment's hesitation, he raised his arms much like his sister and he instantly subconsciously understood what he was doing, he created a massive Red Barrier with a strange blue lightning crackle around it, much like the colour of his left eye.
A Crimson Boundary if you will, a colour that had never been seen in a defensive spell before, as defensive spells were usually either white or blue.
His Crimson Boundary quickly encircled ALL human troops, and any spells that reached it were effectively dispelled.
Gaioz was able to maintain this barrier for an extended period of time, allowing his fellow troops and the supplies they brought to the battlefield to reach the front lines and the wounded to be gathered.
When the Elves realised what was going on, they stopped casting spells and backtracked to their previous positions that they knew were safe.

After keeping the Barrier up for quite a long time, Gaioz succumbed and dropped unconscious to the ground where he was collected and put along with the wounded soldiers in a tent.
Captain Zorad went to the front lines only to witness the first chaos the Elves had wreaked on his troops before noticing the young soldier who used that weird spell and was holding the barrier up on his own. He had his lieutenant find that young soldier and bring him to him as soon as things cooled down a little.
After Gaioz woke up, he saw Christa sitting right beside him on the bed, no one else around besides sleeping wounded soldiers.

"- What was that power? How did I know how to summon it? How did you know?"
"- This was the power that was bestowed upon me from the God of war, which was the seed of power he implanted within our mother."
"- What? How can this be? How did you know how to activate it?"
"- That I cannot answer little brother, I just knew. Just like I just knew that if you followed my movements you would be able to summon it as well. I did not cast that spell, my soul is joined with yours, you are the one summoning it."
"- Yes but how? Once I raised my arms like you it was like I instantly knew how to summon it and did so like it was something natural."
"- All I know is that we need to find out what that power is and how to use it to protect yourself."

Before having the chance to finish their conversation, Captain Zorad's lieutenant barged in and said:

"- I see you're alive and well... Had a nice nap?
"- I was n..."
"- On your feet soldier! The Captain wants to have a word with you, NOW."

He stood up and wore his clothes as Christa disappeared from his sight. He was taken to the main tent, the Captains command headquarters.
Gaioz was questioned about this never-before-seen power he seemed to possess, but even he couldn't explain it; after all, it was the first time he employed a Crimson Boundary, his normal barrier spell that looked like a shell was white & blue, not red. Also, he was pretty shocked too as he wasn't even aware such a power existed or that he could even wield it. And he didn't want to say a word about Christa as they would either think he was crazy, or worse.. Find out that he used a necromancy spell when he was younger to communicate with his dead sister's soul.
Captain Zorad asked his mentor, the King's top advisor, The Grand Meister, for assistance in understanding what that power was and whether they could teach it to the rest of the warriors, because the Elves would have no chance against such a barrier that nullifies spells.
As soon as the Grand Meister received word, he teleported himself to the front lines to see and examine the situation for himself, as he had done before when confronted with such strange power. He had heard stories and legends about these strange Crimson Powers, he also knew that The Church of the 12 considered those that possessed these Crimson Powers as heretics and blasphemers and would usually hunt them down and eliminate them as they considered them a threat to the world. He had never encountered any Crimson Powers as the stories were so obscure that were easily blended in myths and legends from ancient times and were often changed by The Church of the 12 to fit their own agenda.
When they arrived at the border's frontier camp, the Grand Meister insisted on bringing the young soldier to him so he could analyse the spell as well as the caster.
Captain Zorad ordered that Gaioz, who had been detained and was in anti-magic cuffs by that time, as everyone was afraid of this strange power he possessed at the time, be brought immediately to the Grand Meister.
They brought Gaioz in and sat him on a chair in the middle of the room right in front of Captain Zorad and the Grand Meister, with his hands behind his back still locked in anti-magic handcuffs.
They questioned Gaioz about the magic, casting a circle of truth spell to ensure they were getting the truth, and it appeared the young soldier was hiding something and was also avoiding direct questions, about not understanding how he used the spell, as he didn't want them to know about his sister. Because his sister, Christa.
They initially believed he might've been a spy that used this power to infiltrate the army and gain the favour of his superiors by saving those soldiers but after inquiring about it within the circle of truth and Gaioz denied it, they were perplexed as to why he's not answering about certain things and why he's avoiding some subjects intentionally. What was he hiding? They would have to go in an in depth questioning if they wanted answers.
The Grand Meister began inquiring about Gaioz's background to see if he could make any sense of it, but when Gaioz mentioned his mother's name, the Grand Meister's eyes widened in surprise;

"- Andremi you said?! Andremi is still alive? Married and even had a son?!"
"- You know my mother? How do you know her?"

"- Yes, it's a name that I shall not forget, it was the first time I've ever encountered anyone that had lost their magic. I was actually one of the people that were trying to save your mother's life after her tragic accident."
"- You? You were there?"
"- Yes, I was but an apprentice back then but I clearly remember that day... We were called out as there was a tragic accident in Omnitrel and there were 2 survivors that were in critical condition. We rushed there and my commander teleported us to the Healing Centre, none of us were trained for what came next, we didn't know how to help your mother, usually the healing spells use some of the magic in the person's body in order to heal them but.. Your mother had none, or rather, her magic was completely sealed. We had to resort to ancient methods using herbs and bandages in order to try and save her and even then we weren't sure what we were doing."
"- But you did save her, and I'm thankful for that, otherwise I wouldn't be here."
"- Yes, we did. So, you see? I'm not your enemy boy. All I want is to help. I might be the Grand Meister right now but I'm still the same young man that did everything in his power to save that little girl which was your mother."
"- I never said you were my enemy, it's just that... I'm afraid that if I tell you the whole truth, I will either be exiled or sentenced to death. So, I believe it's better for me to keep my mouth shut and do what you will."
"- Exiled or sentenced to death? These are some seriously hard punishments, what might you have done to deserve such a fate? It can't be that bad boy. If you don't tell me, they will hang you as a spy. Unless you are one, I suggest you start telling me your story and I promise you whatever is within my power, which by the way is quite great, to keep you off the noose."

Gaioz then raised his head and looked at him in the eyes, he sensed that he was actually telling the truth and then he remembered that they were within a zone of truth spell, he was definitely telling the truth but what about the Captain? He turned his gaze to the Captain and asked:

"- What about you Captain? Will you help to keep me off the noose if I tell you everything and confirm that I'm not a spy?
"- Boy, you have saved a lot of lives today, my goal is to understand what kind of magic you used and utilize it in order to help save more lives in this terrible war. If you can convince me that you're not a spy, I can guarantee that I'll do everything in my power to keep you off the noose too."
"- Very well then. I shall tell you all I know but I have to warn you both that I don't know much."
"- That is alright, we can figure it out together..."

Said the Grand Meister.

"- It all started ever since I was a little kid, I was born with my twin sister but she unfortunately came into this world as a stillborn. Ever since I can remember, I could see her, right next to me on every step of the way as I was growing up. I could see her growing up with me but no one else could which made me keep quiet about it as I didn't want them to think of me as weird. After I started my studies I came across multiple spells which I managed to master easily but never found one that would allow me to communicate with her as I could see she wanted to speak with me. Then we were taught about a forbidden kind of magic used in the Glaor region, Necromancy..."

Both the Captain and the Grand Meister widened their eyes in surprise.

"- You mean to tell me that you have been seeing your sister's ghost all these years and that you used Necromancy in order to communicate with her ? Why would you do this boy?! There's a reason we forbid the use of Necromancy, it corrupts the spell caster's very essence, their soul to the core. Not to mention that users of Necromancy are often targeted by Demiur for dabbling in his domain of Death and are met with his swift justice."
"- Grand Meister, I wasn't planning on using Necromancy to resurrect her, I only wanted to speak with her and after a lot of research that took a long time, I finally found a spell that might have been able to allow me to speak with her. I went out, gathered all the materials needed for the ritual and cast the Speak With the Dead spell and was able to finally speak with her."
"- How old were you when you performed that ritual?"
"- I don't know, 7 or 8?"
"- 7 or 8? I have seen seasoned spell casters trying to cast the simplest of Necromancy spells and either have them fail miserably or worse, fail and have the Avatar of Death claim their souls... How did you manage to do that at the age of 7 and live to tell the tale?"
"- That's what I was coming to. My sister was not a ghost exactly. At birth, our souls were conjoined and she's a part of me ever since. She still remembers events that happened while we were in our mother's belly and told me everything about it. Unfortunately your guess was right, that Crimson Barrier I used was a forbidden power that The Church of the 12 considers blasphemy and they would surely label me a heretic for using it. It was the Power of Malekus, the

God of War."
"- The God of War? What does Malekus have anything to do with it?"
"- From what my sister told me, when our mother was on the verge of death, she met Malekus and he injected some of his power within our mother, sealing her magic and giving her off springs the ability to use a fraction of his power once they were born. That Crimson Barrier was supposed to be my sister's power, she showed me how to access the power and use it to save myself and the rest of the soldiers on the battlefield."
"- Do you mean to tell me that both you and your sister were supposed to have a power like that and that your mother's sealed magical powers were a result of the Power of Malekus?"
"- As I said, I don't know for sure, I am speculating and going by what my sister has told me so far."
"- That is a lot to take in but at least we know you're telling us the truth. And I will keep my word, I will do anything within my power to keep you off the noose and even more, I'll try to negotiate with The Church of 12 in order to gain their favour on the matter and not have them send their head-hunters against you, after all now you're a soldier of Omnitrel who has saved quite a few lives and if you can control this power, you will certainly be a huge asset to this war against the Elves. I'm sure our King will be able to see it this way too."
"- I will take your word for it, as for controlling it. I can, but it takes every ounce of Power I have from my body, strangely enough it doesn't deplete my Magical power, it depletes my stamina."
"- Well, that is certainly strange, with your permission I would like to keep a close eye and be updated on everything that is related to this power to record it."

He turns to Captain Zorad and says:

"- Set him free, I entrust him under your command but remember, he's not just a solder, he might be the key to ending this war."
"- Do not worry, I will take good care of him, if you'd like to stay to record his progress, I have already set up a tent for you next to mine."

Said Captain Zorad as he unlocked Gaioz's handcuffs.

"- Corporal! Get in here!"

The corporal that was standing outside the headquarters tent barged in, stood in attention and shouted:

"- Yes Captain! Your orders, Sir?"
"- Take Gaioz here, give him a uniform, feed him and brief him in our current position and how the war has been going on thus far, tomorrow he'll be joining a team I'm putting together."
"- Yes Captain! Immediately!"

Gaioz stood up and followed the Corporal out of the tent, as they headed out he noticed that it was already dark, he had been unconscious for the whole day as he arrived at the battlefield at first light. They moved through the camp and he was taken to another big tent at the back end of the camp. As they entered he noticed a lot of tables and chairs and quite a few soldiers eating and drinking after a hard day on the battlefield.

"- Sit here, I'll go see what's left of food, we're a bit late so you'll have to make due with whatever's left."
"- I don't mind, I'll sit right over here."

The Corporal went through and moved in the back end of what seemed to be a field kitchen that they prepared the food for all the soldiers. Gaioz sat on the closest table to him while Christa appeared and sat with him, he looked around and he could see mostly veteran soldiers drinking in groups and noticed that almost all of them had a certain sign sewn on the arm of their armour, not all signs were the same but he figured that this might be a way to tell apart each squad. Before even finishing the thought, he felt a slap on the back and as he turned around he saw one of the seasoned soldiers that was sitting near the entrance of the tent, him and his buddies were all around him inspecting him from top to bottom as he said:

"- So, what are you supposed to be? A civilian in the war camp?"
"- No, he's the guy that they had in the stretcher in handcuffs, are you some tree-hugger Elf lover boy?"
"- Handcuffs? Do we have a traitor in our midst boys? Shall we show him what we do to tree-huggers and Elves?"

Gaioz did not seem phased by the empty threats, sure it would be an uneven fight if he went up against 5 veterans but he chose to remain calm and try to de-escalate the situation.

"- Guys, It was a misunderstanding, I resolved it with Captain Zorad and the Grand Meister and they've just sent me here to eat something, go grab my uniform and that's it."

The guy In front of him grabbed him by his shirt and raised him up pulling his other hand back and preparing a fire spell by the looks of it saying:

"- Are you implying that we're wrong, tree-hugger? What do you say boys, do you want to see up close what happens when a tree-hugger catches fire?"
"- Can we please not do this? I really don't want to get into any trouble on my first day guys."
"- Well, seems you're out of luck tree-hugger! Your buddies killed my friends 2 days ago, somebody has to pay!"

As soon as he finished this sentence, he threw a punch at Gaioz along with the fire spell he had prepared, Gaioz blocked his hand and saw Christa showing him a move right behind the soldier and by tried to hear what she was saying but he couldn't as the commotion started by the soldiers all around him, he managed to read her lips and she was saying "try to imagine a barrier around your body!".
After the first punch being blocked, the soldier was furious and readied another spell and at the same time slammed Gaioz on the table and threw a second punch along with a second fire spell but Gaioz had time to focus and try out what his sister suggested and as soon as the fire spell was to touch him it dissipated and fizzled out of his attackers hand but he still took the punch in the face.
At this point the Corporal came out of the kitchen and witnessed the soldiers being gathered around a table and as he moved closer he saw Gaioz being held down at the table, face down getting punch after punch at this point but all the punches that carried spells on them, fizzled out on impact which made the soldiers a bit anxious and worried.

"- What the fuck is going on here?!"

Shouted the Corporal as he moved closer and grabbed the attackers arm, and with a swift motion throwing him on the other side of the tent

"- What has gotten into all of you? Direct this anger towards the Elves, not allies!"
"- But Sergeant! We saw him in cuffs a few hours ago! Who is he? Is he a prisoner? A tree-hugger?"
"- What are you on about? Even if he was, you attack kids now? He's 17... What's the matter with you? And no, as far as I know he's not an enemy, he's supposed to join a special squad tomorrow that the Captain is creating, if anyone messes with him again, you'll have to answer to the Captain."

As he said that, the soldiers seemed less motivated to mess with Gaioz. The Sergeant picked him up and took a look at his face, his nose was bleeding but he was smiling.

"- You got your ass kicked, why are you freaking smiling?"
"- Can you please give a message to the Captain for me? Tell him "I managed to control it perfectly!", he'll understand."
"- Ok, let's get you cleaned up and get you something to eat, the chef has a few things left."

At the same time at the other side of the War camp, the Grand Meister and Captain Zorad had a different kind of conversation.

"- I can't believe that Andremi is his mother! The little girl he had saved all those years ago, the one who had lost her ability to use magic, had a son, and her son possessed such incredible power!"
"- Do you really think that this kid will be enough to win this crazy war? We've already seen the nullifying properties of his power but he's a kid, he doesn't even know if he can control it or if he can even sustain it, you heard what he said... it depleted all his stamina for that short time and he was out cold for nearly 10 hours."
"- Yes, you are correct. But as we both know, every new spell, any new power becomes easier to use with practice. If we are to believe him, it was the first time he ever used this power. I believe that given time he will be able to master it, control it and sustain it for longer periods of time."
"- I hope you're right. So, what is your plan about The Church of the 12? Do you even have a plan?"
"- Yes, I know the head of the Church. We go way back. I will go and personally talk to him tomorrow morning, I will tell him that I'm taking this boy under my wing if need be and that he's going to be under my protection and I'll be directly responsible for his actions. I just hope I'm not wrong about him."
"- Are you sure? They are a huge organization, they might try to label you a collaborator of a heretic if yo..."

"- Yes I am sure, do you forget who you're talking to? They're not the only ones with authority! Besides, I'll speak to the King about the situation first, I will make sure that I have his support before going forward with this and then act, it seems to be a VERY delicate matter."

As soon as he finished his sentence, a soldier came in

"- Sir! I have an urgent message from Sergeant Keland."
"- Ok, out with it then! Do you expect a special invitation?"
"- His message is "The boy was able to completely control it", that's it sir."

Both men looked at each other before Captain Zorad saying:

"- Thank you soldier, dismissed!"
"- Sir, Yes Sir!"

He left the tent as both the Grand Meister and Captain Zorad seemed very excited by those news.

"- How did he manage to already control it?
"- It seems I was right, at least now I have something positive to tell the King while asking for his approval on the matter."
"- Well, I don't know what to say, that boy just managed to put our minds at ease. How did he manage to control it though, did something happen? Oh well, I'll inquire about it tomorrow, I'm too tired for that now. Goodnight Master."
"- Goodnight, I'm going to take my rest and teleport tomorrow to the Capital to meet the King and make the necessary arrangements for our young friend."

As the Grand Meister withdrew to his tent, he thought back to the time that he was just an apprentice in the Dwarven Kingdom of Queattin, he remembered reading in ancient texts about people who lost their ability to use magic after being on the verge of death and then were brought back to life seemingly without their magical prowess, and some of them were eventually driven insane. The descendants of those people would be able to develop terrifying abilities. The Crimson Boundary was the name given to this ability rather than a spell. He remembered reading about it in the same Dwarven texts, how at its peak of power it could envelop an entire continent in its Crimson Veil. It was said to have been wielded by an Elven General Thousands of years ago, at the start of the Great Conflict of Celestials and Demons and it was said to be what protected the Elven Kingdom from those forces.
He cast a memory recall spell and remembered clearly reading about this ability "A Red Barrier envelops the user, preventing hostile entities from passing through and nullifying their magic to the core. If a magic user passes through it, they will be unable to cast magic while inside; it acts as an anti-magic zone around the user, but the user will still be able to use magic without consequence."
What kind of young boy could wield such power? Was it related to his mother's injury and subsequent loss of magical abilities years before?
He was going to leave with even more questions, despite the fact that he had managed to answer a couple.
Captain Zorad decided to take Gaioz and train him personally, to his surprise Gaioz was a very skilled fighter and very intelligent. He managed to soak up years of tactical battlefield knowledge that Captain Zorad had within days and progress with his physical and Crimson Barrier training exceeding expectations.
After seeing that he was as ready as he could be for live combat, Captain Zorad would go ahead and upgrade Gaioz's' status to Corporal 1st class and put him on the front lines with a special squad of spell casters that he put together, most of them seasoned veterans, all masters in their respective specialty. Their squad would be responsible for infiltrating enemy lines and sabotaging them with a goal to cause them such distress that the Elves would have to withdraw from their positions as the Omnitrellian forces would gain ground.
In the meanwhile the Grand Meister did as he said and early in the morning he set out towards the Capital and teleported straight to his chambers. He sought an audience with the King who at the time was consulting with his 2 generals about the army positions and how they would best defend the Capital if it came to that.

"- My King, I have some news that will definitely interest you!"
"- Kaelan, where were you? Did you just get back from the battlefield?"
"- Yes, I spend the night there, Zorad was kind enough to let me use one of the officer tents. Never mind that though, I have news and matters to discuss my King, privately if possible."
"- Well, You heard him gentlemen, I trust that you know your way out."
"- My King! With all due respect! We haven't concluded to a course of action!"

"- You are right, I will convene with my personal advisor and come up with a strategy. Are there any objections to that?"
"- Of course not my King."

The two Generals bow and turn around moving towards the exit.
As soon as they get out of the War Hall, the Grand Meister approaches the King and says:

"- Well look at you! Commanding Generals 20 years older than you with ease! Much like your late father. Very good Aleister!"
"- I've learned from the best, you and my father were my greatest teachers, I would be a fool not to put in use what I've learned now that I am the King. So, what was it that you wished to talk to me about, did something happen?"
"- Oh yes... Something did happen and I will need the Crown's assistance on the matter... And if all goes well, we might not only finish this war but win it. We know that the Elves are superior spell casters unfortunately which is what gives them the edge on the battlefield and how they've cornered us up until now."
"- Get to the point my good man! What is the matter that need the Crown's assistance and how can we turn the war and win it?!"
"- Do you remember a tale I told you when you were little? About an Elven General that had a mysterious Crimson Power and managed to push back Celestials and Demons by protecting the Capital of the Elven Kingdom along with all surrounding cities with a Barrier Spell ?"
"- I think I do but what does that have to do with anything?"
"- You'll see where I'm getting at, let me finish."
"- Alright, I'll play along. Please, continue..."
"- You are aware that The Church of the 12 are actively hunting down individuals that appear to have some sort of strange magic and labels them Heretics, Blasphemers and Traitors, correct ?"
"- Yes, not that I condone such acts but my father allowed it while he was King as he didn't see any benefit in going against the Church of the 12 and thought they knew more on the matter."
"- Well, I have a reason for the current King to put a stop to it. There is a young man, currently serving in the front lines under Captain Zorad which has exhibited a strange Crimson Power. Captain Zorad informed me that their supply vehicles and troop transports got ambushed and were being hammered by a barrage of spells from Elven forces until that young man raised a Crimson Barrier that nullified their spells on contact, giving time to our forces to move to safety, shortly after he collapsed and was dragged out of the battlefield to rest. After he woke up I had a chat with him in which I had already cast a Zone of Truth spell to ensure that I will gain credible and true information out of him. He admitted to having cast a forbidden spell when he was younger that would allow him to speak with his sister's ghost, as his soul is conjoined with his sister's for some reason and ever since he was little he could see her. His sister's ghost explained how he could use that power and after she did, he activated it and protected the rest of our troops till they got to safety."
"- And you believe him?"
"- Actually, yes I do, I knew his mother and her story was a peculiar one...

The Grand Meister goes on to recount the story of Andremi and whatever else he found out from Gaioz while he was talking with him to the King, who after listening to these stories became very intrigued and wanted to meet Gaioz in person. A Royal order was sent to The Church of the 12 that Gaioz was a royal soldier that would answer only to the King and if any action was to be taken against him, it would be labelled as treason and The Church of the 12 would lose all rights within the Kingdom of Omnitrel. The Grand Meister was tasked to take it to the Head of the Church of the 12 as they were once brothers in arms and he would have more diplomacy with him.

After the deed was drafted by the King and the Grand Meister, he made his way to the Church of the 12, in the heart of Omnitrel. Making his way in, he requested an audience with the Grand Priest and awaited.
Shortly after the Grand Meister was guided into the Church where the Grand Priest awaited him in his chambers.

"- Kaelan! Been a long time old friend. What brings you here today?"
"- Thank you for agreeing to meet me on such short notice Limaver. I am afraid that I'm bit here on a casual visit or to reminisce about old times. I bring a letter, or deed if you will from the King himself."
"- A deed from the King? For the Church? What kind of deed?"
"- As you know we're at war, I was informed by Captain Zorad, an old student of mine who commands our forces on the battlefield that there was an individual that exhibited some strange power."
"- Strange power? You seriously don't mean...."
"- I'm afraid I do old friend. I met the individual myself, he's just a boy, 17 years old. I can't go into much detail about it but after consulting with the King and presenting my report, the King has declared that this boy is to be protected

under the Crown's orders and anyone who might wish to harm him will be labelled as traitors."
"- Does this boy possess the Cursed Crimson Power? If so, you bring me in a very difficult position."
"- Yes he does. And that is the reason I personally wanted to deliver this deed to you. Limaver, I have spoken with the child, I even cast a Zone of Truth spell in order to prevent him lying to me. He is of no threat to anyone, well.. Except the Elves of course as the King intends to use him as a weapon against them and that is the reason for the deed."
"- What kind of Cursed Power has this child exhibited?"
"- You might be glad to hear that it is not an offensive Power rather a defensive one."
"- What do you mean? Almost all the Cursed Crimson Powers we have ever encountered either mimicked the results of highly powerful offensive spells or enchanted the users body to great lengths to make them an essential killing machine."
"- Well, his is not of that short. He has the power to create a Crimson Barrier around him and his allies, when he first used this power it was to protect himself and 50 wounded soldiers from a barrage of offensive spells from the Elven forces that were targeting our troop and resupply line."
"- Very well, I do trust you and the King in your judgement and take no action against him, I will put him under surveillance though and if he ever becomes a threat to the Realm, I will ask the order from the King to eliminate him."
"- Thank you old friend, I will relay your reply to our King."

In the meantime, back on the battlefield, after a week of rigorous training, Gaioz eventually learned to use his Crimson Boundary as he came to call it at will after many tests and trials, but after training him for a week and seeing how his power gets activated, without any sort of incantation or hand gestures, Captain Zorad concluded that they couldn't hope to recreate the power he possessed because it appeared to be an inherent ability.

At this point, the only option is to send him as planned behind enemy lines and hope that he can protect his squad and thwart the Elven Kingdom's daily assaults. His squad would have to use mundane means of warfare because they knew that Gaioz's Crimson Boundary would prevent anyone within his Barrier power from casting magic except Gaioz himself.
To protect their borders, the Humans used machinations purchased from the Dwarven Kingdom of Queattin that used the powers of Omnium Crystals to fire large bolts of fire at their enemies, decimating them. These massive bolts of fire would be easily deflected by a simple shielding spell, but with the Crimson Boundary in place, no one could cast such a spell. So Gaioz's squad would have to be at the heart of the enemy positions, activate his Crimson Boundary and take out any defensive spell casters in the area so that the assault could take place. Then they would have to find a way to clear out of the way so that they won't get caught in friendly fire. Not an easy task for sure but Captain Zorad had faith that his soldiers could pull it off. And so the operation began, Gaioz and his squad which had 6 members in total including him, made their way to the enemy base in the dead of night with Gaioz activating a small anti-magic barrier around them to prevent enemy spells to detect them.
They successfully infiltrated the enemy base by assassinating their lookouts and managing to find the positions of their defensive spell casters. Within the span of an hour, Gaioz cast a messaging spell towards Captain Zorad and informed him that their mission was successful and that they could go ahead and start the assault as they were getting clear of the Elven base.
The Humans were able to advance from their positions and go from being outnumbered on the defensive to going on the offensive and decimating their opponents. Even though The Crimson Boundary was winning the war, Gaioz informed Captain Zorad that his power was not infinite and that he could only use it a few times per day depending on the area he had to cover and the time he had to keep the Barrier up.
They needed to devise a strategy to end the war as soon as possible, after 5 years of hard battles and guerrilla tactics, the Humans managed to drive the Elves back to the Shim'Lar Lakes, where they would hold their ground, and sent an emissary to the Elves, requesting a meeting between the two sides.
The Elven Commander on the other hand, remembered reading about the Crimson Boundary in his studies after witnessing it for the first time. It was the power of Alaev, their Great General and the Creator of their Kingdom.
Alaev lived 40 thousand years ago and was the creator of Kylles'ar as well as the entire Kingdom of the Elves. He was the one who exiled the Dark Elves to the Underground Kingdom of Lum'Uzet for using Necromancy. They knew they didn't have much of a choice with the power of the Crimson Boundary against them, so they agreed to meet with the Humans.
The two sides met on a small island in the Shim'Lar lakes, where they talked and agreed to a cease-fire and the establishment of new borders (Because the Elves knew that if the war went on, they would lose more lands to the Humans, and the Humans would not relinquish the lands they had conquered).
After five years of difficult and arduous fighting, the war was finally won, the Elves were pushed back further into their region, the human kingdom gained more land, and a treaty, The Shim'Lar Treaty, was forged.

www.ingramcontent.com/pod-product-compliance
Lightning Source LLC
LaVergne TN
LVHW041304150826
845673LV00008B/2727

* 9 7 9 8 3 7 4 6 5 6 8 7 9 *